Hedge

Over

Heels

Elise McMullen-Ciotti

SCHOLASTIC INC.

All rights reserved. Published by Scholastic Inc., *Publishers since 1920*. SCHOLASTIC and associated logos are trademarks and/or registered trademarks of Scholastic Inc.

The publisher does not have any control over and does not assume any responsibility for author or third-party websites or their content.

This book is a work of fiction. Names, characters, places, and incidents are either the product of the author's imagination or are used fictitiously, and any resemblance to actual persons, living or dead, business establishments, events, or locales is entirely coincidental.

ISBN 978-1-338-81046-2

10 9 8 7 6 5 4 3 2 1   22 23 24 25 26

Printed in the U.S.A.   40
First printing 2022

Book design by Omou Barry

To all my chickens—you know who you are ;)

1

No matter where you live in the US, school buses are all the same. Same yellow paint. Same crazy smell of vinyl and sneakers. The same slightly sticky floor. The same unused seat belts. Kids are either screaming at each other or they're being as silent as the grave with only the sound of the road beneath them.

A school bus is a school bus is a school bus.

The only thing that changed for me was the view outside the school bus window. Last school year, and even last week, the view out the window had been palm trees, faded buildings, and the bright sun rising from the blue-green ocean in Pensacola, Florida. The year before that, the window was filled with the lush green oak trees of Augusta, Georgia, with its wide yards and a big river running through town.

Now the view from the school bus window was Frederick, Maryland. I wasn't happy about it.

It was my first day at a new school and it was *Friday*. Seriously, who starts at a new school on a Friday? Plus, beginning seventh grade in October after everyone else had already started wasn't exactly going to be fun. It was going to be messy. I was doomed to stick out like a bright red cardinal in a sea of angry blue jays. But there was nothing I could do about it. The US Army dictated just about everything in my life, including when and where I moved. Thanks, Army.

When the bus stopped, a kid with bright purple glasses and a mouthful of gum climbed the steps and headed straight to the back. His sneakers made a sticky, squeaky sound as they passed.

Exactly, I thought. *Sticky.*

I looked back out the window. A colorful mural peeked around the corner of a diner. I hated to admit it, but Frederick, Maryland, looked kinda nice. I could even say that it was downright *artsy*. There was a beautiful canal downtown crossed by small bridges and filled with water lilies. Aunty Jacq was going to love that. Each bridge looked unique, with colorful mosaics on its walls or ornate railings along its arches.

I tried to peer inside the mom-and-pop shops we passed—bakeries and coffee shops that bustled with early morning activity. We rounded a corner and shuttled down a street alongside a large green park where an outdoor theater with bright yellow seats sat waiting for an audience. A man jogged along one of the park trails with a beautiful collie as another couple played with a corgi puppy.

Wait! I lit up from the inside out. There were dog people in Frederick! I would love to be one of those. Go for walks in the park with my dog. Play Frisbee with my dog. Of course, I'd have to finally, for-the-love-of-all-things-cute, be allowed to have a dog, but it was only a matter of time.

Yep. Frederick seemed like a real nice town. But all of a sudden, the pit of my stomach turned sour. Who knew how long I'd get to stay in this nice town?

Aunty Jacq—that's short for Jacqueline—had suggested we move to Frederick instead of the army base in Fort Meade. She's my mom's older sister and has lived with us ever since I was born. To be honest, sometimes Aunty Jacq feels more like a mom to me than my mom. Don't get me wrong, I love my mom. It's just that she's a Sergeant First Class and that means sometimes she isn't around.

Thankfully, I had picked the perfect seat on the bus—the seat right behind the driver. No one ever wanted to sit near the driver and that always left a big gap of empty seats between me and the rest of the kids on the bus. It was better that way. There was no reason to try to be social. Like I said before, I didn't know how long I'd even be in the town, let alone at this school.

I'd been moving from place to place and school to school ever since second grade. The army assigned my mom to live where they needed her, and then they'd send her on missions to who knows where for months at a time. That meant me and Aunty Jacq were sometimes left behind in a strange new place, trying to adjust but never quite fitting in. I hated it. I mean, I was really proud of my mom. I just wished we could finally stay put somewhere. That the army could need her to stay somewhere—anywhere—with me.

The school bus stopped and four students climbed on. They were a quiet bunch and grabbed some seats six or seven rows behind me. *Good.* If I just scowled enough, maybe no one would try to sit with me.

But just as the bus doors started to close, a kid younger than me huffed up the stairs. He lingered near the front, looking at me like I'd stolen his seat.

Forget it, I thought, looking out the front window. *First come, first served, buddy. First come, first served.*

The kid finally accepted defeat and sat on the other side of the aisle, but continued to stare. I did my best to ignore him, watching the road as we drove on. The bus driver eyed me from his review mirror every once in a while, but I pretended not to see him either.

That morning, Aunty Jacq and Mom had been so overly cheery as I'd headed out the door, I nearly told them to eat worms. Couldn't they tell I wasn't in the best of moods? That being dropped into an ocean of cruel twelve-year-olds who were waiting to eat me alive wasn't exactly my idea of fun?

They'd said to have a good day.

Impossible.

They'd said I'd get to take an art class, so I'd probably like this school better than the others I'd gone to.

Sure. Yeah. Right.

They'd also said it wouldn't kill me to make a few friends.

Nope. Not going to happen. Not after being ghosted by so-called friends in Pensacola. Not after bawling my eyes out when I'd had to leave my fourth-grade BFF in Augusta. I couldn't go through all that again.

The only friend I planned to make this year was of the cute, tail-wagging, four-legged variety. Dogs could move with you. Protect you. Fetch. Roll over. But most important, they knew how to stay. Dogs didn't promise to write. And they didn't forget you. Ever.

2

Purple. It was purple inside Frederick Middle School. It had to be the most Halloween-y school I'd ever walked into. From top to bottom, the walls were swathed in violet and orange Halloween decor. I wanted to hate how cheesy it was. I really did. But Halloween, All Souls' Day, and the Day of the Dead were my favorite holidays. So the bats hanging from the ceilings, skeletons on the lockers, and tombstones and ghosts on every bulletin board were something I could get behind. I tried to look bored by it all. I really did. But a smile stretched across my face as I felt a crackle of excitement in the air.

Truth was, I'd always been a bit macabre. If something

had skulls on it, I liked it. I craved funny, spooky stories that made you laugh and jump out of your chair, like *Beetlejuice* and *Coco*. *The Nightmare Before Christmas* was my favorite Christmas movie of all time. There was just something about it. Skeletons rocked.

I looked down at my skull-covered Converse high-tops. I'd painted them myself. *I can do this,* I told myself. *I can.*

I stood up a little straighter and headed toward the main office. As I opened the glass doors, a student pushed through them, knocking me backward.

"Sorry!" he said, his feet pounding the floor with screeches.

"Sure," I said, resituating my book bag.

Inside the office, a girl about my age sat on a stool behind the counter. She had strawberry blonde hair and green glasses that pointed catlike up to her temples. A name tag pinned onto her sweater read STUDENT ASSISTANT.

"How can I help you?" she asked with her strawberry hair bouncing around her face. Then she leaned forward, looking at me more closely while pushing up her glasses. "Are you new? I'm not sure we've met. I'm Marcie Peterson, the first-period student assistant."

"Yes, I'm new," I said, looking around to make sure there wasn't anyone else around me. "It's my first day."

"Oh, that's great! You'll love FMS! Where did you move from?"

"Pensacola," I said, praying she didn't ask more questions.

"With the beach that has the nesting turtles?" she asked, sitting higher on her stool.

"Uh . . . yeah. I think so," I said.

"That's amazing! Hold on, let me get your paperwork from Ms. Abbot. What's your name?"

"Rayna. Rayna Snow."

"Like the weather?" Marcie asked quizzically.

I couldn't believe that was still following me around. Ever since I was little, kids had turned my name into "Rain and Snow." I just stood there looking at her with zero expression on my face until she stopped waiting for a response.

"Hold on, I'll get Ms. Abbot."

I nodded, taking a moment to set my bag down and look around the room. It was different than my other schools' offices. It was . . . bright. Two large windows along the back wall let in the morning light. Some adults were laughing inside an office somewhere. The Halloween theme hadn't stopped outside the office door. A jack-o'-lantern sat on the counter surrounded by arching black-cat figurines. Orange and purple lights hung around the inner office doors.

Marcie sprang back a few minutes later with some papers in her hand. "I see now, I'm sorry. It's Ray-*nah* L. Snow. Seventh grade." She slid the papers in front of me. "This is a copy of your schedule, and this is a map of the school with room numbers. It looks like we're in the same science class, so that's cool."

She looked up and smiled. I just raised my eyebrows.

"And you have Mr. Toliver for social studies and homeroom. The bell hasn't rung yet, but you could probably go on down there and see if the room is open. Oh! And here is your locker number. Probably the most important thing! It's three-one-four. Like the number pi. Seventh-grade lockers are all in the east wing, so I'm sure I'll see you around!" she concluded, smiling.

"Thanks," I said, giving her my courteous half smile that always seemed to pacify strangers. Even when I didn't feel it at all. I grabbed my backpack and headed for the door.

"Oh, by the way," Marcie called. "I love your hair. Such a deep purple! It's so good to see someone in the Halloween spirit."

Courteous half smile again, and I was out the door. I wasn't about to explain that the color wasn't for Halloween, but just what I liked. My three favorite colors, perfect to cover dark brown hair and go with green eyes: deep concord purple, crimson red, and blackest black.

After searching for my homeroom for what felt like forever, I realized I must have made a wrong turn somewhere. I looked down at my map. Yep. I'd ended up at the opposite side of the school. I turned around and headed the other way. And that's when I saw it: the reason for all the anticipation in the air. A big painted sign read:

FMS HALLOWEEN EXTRAVAGANZA!

I read the details. Haunted house in the gym, treats and games for all ages in the cafeteria. Trick-or-treating in every classroom. It was a whole family affair. As much as I loved Halloween, I probably wouldn't go. I mean, especially not if my mom wasn't in town. Maybe I'd go anyway? No. Probably not. But maybe. Jeez.

As I hustled toward Mr. Toliver's room in the south wing, the paper bats and the ghosts lining the hallway seemed to cackle at me, chiming in on my confusion. "She should go! No, she shouldn't! Not alone. Of course alone!"

Shut up! I silently screamed, rounding the corner to finally find room 248, Mr. Toliver—Social Studies.

The face of a middle-aged man who had to be my new homeroom teacher turned to catch me frozen in the doorway. *Deep breath, Rayna. Deep breath.*

3

Morning light shone through the windows, casting a cheery glow about the place, like the classrooms you see in the movies. The room was quiet, and I let it wash over me. Not only had the hallway decorations gone silent, but I was also happy to find no other students in the classroom. Five rows of empty desks stretched neatly from the front of the room near the teacher's desk to the back wall, which was dotted with coat hooks. There was an actual chalkboard at the front. *Wow.* I hadn't seen one of those in a while. My previous schools had white dry-erase boards or SMART Boards.

"Good morning," the man said from behind the teacher's

desk as he looked at me looking at the chalkboard.

I knew I couldn't stay silent forever. "Oh. Um. Hello. Are you Mr. Toliver?"

"I sure hope so," he said, smiling, "or my students won't learn a lick of history today."

I gave him a blank stare for a second, taking that in. Right. Courteous half grin. "Yes. Um. I'm Rayna Snow. I'm your new homeroom student," I said, approaching the desk.

"Ah yes," he said. "Welcome to FMS. Principal Stewart let me know you were coming this week. But when I didn't see you on Monday, I thought maybe she was mistaken."

"I know. Starting on a Friday is . . . kind of weird," I said, looking down at the little skulls on my shoes for strength.

"Nonsense," he said. "New beginnings arrive when they're meant to, not when they're planned."

I looked back up at him. "Sir, would it be all right if I asked you for a favor this morning?"

"Sure," he said, leaning back in his chair.

I lifted my chin a little higher. "Would you please not announce to the class that I'm new and this is my first day?" I asked. I studied his reaction while I waited for the answer. He didn't know it, but this was more than a favor. It was a test. If he wouldn't respect my request, then I knew what kind of teacher I had—one who didn't care at all about kids who moved around a lot or how they felt.

Understanding seemed to emanate from Mr. Toliver's warm amber eyes. His small, neat mustache matched his soft heather-gray hair. He reminded me of one of those comfy cardigan sweaters with the elbow patches.

Mr. Toliver smiled. "Of course, Rayna. No problem at all."

My whole body filled with relief. Maybe the first day would be okay.

"I would like to introduce you to at least one student, someone who could share some notes with you so you can get up to speed in the class. Would that be okay?"

I nodded. I hated to admit it, but Mr. Toliver was right. I needed some help if I was going to keep getting those beautiful spiky As on my report card. I found a seat in the back row by the windows as the bell rang and students began filing into the classroom.

Just when I thought that the seat in front of me would remain empty, I noticed a boy quickly making his way in my direction. He wore an army-green jacket over a long-sleeved T-shirt that sported a hand making a peace sign on its front. A long chocolate-brown braid reached down past his chest, and his turquoise eyes made my breath catch. He smiled at me as he sat down. I gave nothing away—at least I tried not to.

What was wrong with me? Who cared if there was a cute human sitting at the desk in front of me? I had a more important mission to execute:

- Make all As.
- Convince Mom a dog was absolutely necessary.
- Get through this new school year without too much pain. (Meaning, avoid making friends!!!)

Mr. Toliver passed out printouts that read "The Influence of African Culture in America" at the top, and the hour passed quickly. Turned out, he was a good storyteller, and Africa was pretty amazing. I had no idea that it had fifty-four countries, over two thousand languages, and that okra, watermelon, yams, and black-eyed peas all came from there. And it had definitely influenced the culture down South, especially the restaurants. But I wasn't about to raise my hand and share that fact with the class.

When the bell rang, I packed up slowly and waited. If everyone left before me, then I'd have better luck going unnoticed. I situated everything neatly in my backpack and stood up, adjusting my sweater. Then I put my head down and walked quickly past Mr. Toliver, who leaned against his desk, talking to peace-T-shirt boy.

"Rayna, hang on a second," Mr. Toliver called out.

I froze.

"I'd like for you to meet Nick Smallwood."

"Hey," Nick said, flashing his smile again.

I looked at them both, my face as blank as I could make it, and said nothing.

"Rayna, Nick is going to lend you his notes on Unit One to help you get caught up in class, okay?"

"Oh, um, sure," I said. "Thank you." I glanced up at Nick, but the warmth in his gaze had me staring at the floor again. "I probably should—"

"Nick also tutors sixth graders after school a few times each week, so he's got the makings of a great teacher someday," Mr. Toliver said, his warm-cardigan grin gleaming.

I looked at them, searching in my brain for polite things to say.

"I'll walk you out," Nick said once he realized that no words would be coming out of me any time soon. "See you Monday, Mr. Toliver," he said, and motioned for me to follow him.

In the hallway, I was about to bolt when Nick gently grabbed my backpack.

"Wait. Hold on," he said, chuckling.

"Yes," I said coolly, like everything was completely normal.

"What's your number? We could set up a time to meet if you want and go over Unit One."

"Oh, um, I do have a phone. But not like yours, probably. My mom's in the army, does cybersecurity, and has ruled out any and all smartphones from my life. Instead I have this 'dumb' phone, at least that's what they call it, so I'm not online on it or anything or on social media, but it can text or call, and be tracked by my mom and only my mom," I said. *Oh no. I'm beginning to ramble.* "So I'm not sure if I can give you the number? I'd have to ask, I guess? I mean, I'm sure she'll be fine, 'cause it's for social studies, but you know, I should ask."

"So you do talk." Nick grinned, swinging his backpack

around to the front of his chest and pulling out a notebook and pen. He wrote his name and number on a piece of paper. "It's totally cool. We can be old-school, no problem," he said, tearing the paper from the notebook and holding it out to me. "I have some time Monday after school. Let me know?"

I grabbed the paper from his hand. "Sure, of course. Thanks."

Courteous half smile.

And then I was gone down the purple-and-orange hallway with my heart beating in my ears.

4

Why was it that the ride to school in the morning took no time at all, but the one home lasted an absolute eternity? Aunty Jacq would chalk it up to "youthful impatience," as she liked to call it. But I thought it was more like the Doctor from *Doctor Who* playing a joke on middle schoolers.

When the bus finally stopped at the end of my new street, I pretended to drop something on the floor. Just like after class, I let everyone else make their way off the bus first, avoiding all eye contact. Then I zipped out of the yellow box like lightning.

Compared to where we'd lived before, Camden Lane was really nice. The bus stop was at the top of a small hill, and my street meandered down from it, creating its own little valley. The houses on each side weren't too nice or too broken-down—kind of right in the middle. Most were brick with friendly porches that sported their own unique style, but they still looked like they all belonged together. There were also some pretty impressive trees.

As I studied the turrets of a particularly cute Victorian and the cobwebs strung all over its banisters, I nearly missed the cluster of four kids up ahead. I recognized one of them. It was the girl from the office, Marcie. I hung back, but couldn't help overhearing their conversation. Two Black boys with short, cropped hair and oddly similar backpacks—one blue with green trim, and the other green with blue trim—were arguing as Marcie listened. A girl wearing a bright neon-pink T-shirt and cool ripped-up jeans began drifting away from the pack.

"We should tell her and tell her quick," Blue Backpack said.

"No way," Green Backpack said. "Don't you remember the last time Mom went up to the school?"

"Yeah, but you know she doesn't—"

"—like for us to do science projects—"

"—together," they said in unison.

"Why doesn't she like you working together?" Marcie asked.

"Because we end up arguing," said Blue.

"He leaves everything for me to do," said Green.

"Not true."

"True."

"Not."

"Oh, that's right, like the banana-ripening experiment in fourth grade," Marcie concurred.

"Exactly," both boys said.

"Well, I have to agree with Kevin," she said. "If all you're going to do is argue about it, you could get a worse grade. Maybe it's better to let your mom ask Mrs. Castaneda to assign you other partners. Just be honest. It's always best to be honest."

"Data is data," Blue said.

"Facts are facts," Marcie agreed.

All of a sudden, Blue Backpack noticed me out of the corner of his eye. He turned and gave me a head nod, tapping his brother on the arm, who did the same. They were twins. Marcie recognized me and waved.

Please don't slow down. I gave my polite half smile, then looked down at my shoes. *Good idea*, I told them silently. I bent down and retied my perfectly tied shoes, letting the group drift away down the street. When I stood up, the boys were laughing as they walked up the steps of the Victorian. Marcie and the pink T-shirt girl were nowhere to be found. I was glad they hadn't stopped.

Five minutes later, I slid into the foyer of my-house-that-didn't-feel-like-a-home, to find a newly hung coatrack staring back at me. *Yes! The movers came!* Boxes were piled everywhere, creating narrow trails that were tricky to navigate. But the house was full of light and much bigger than anywhere we'd lived as we'd moved from base to base, from military home to military home.

A toasty, buttery, and sweet aroma met my nose. *Shortbreads!* Aunty Jacq must have already found her baking pans. I quickly headed toward the kitchen.

"What were you thinking?" I heard Aunty Jacq ask.

I stopped short before entering. Something was wrong.

"I'm sorry to say it, Kate, but Rayna's going to hate the idea."

I frowned and stepped into the room. "What idea am I going to hate?"

5

"Rayna! You're home. I didn't hear you come in. How was your first day? Did you like any of your teachers?"

I was about to answer but my mom kept talking. "So I was thinking, tomorrow is Saturday, and the weather looks good."

Where is she going with this?

"I decided it's the perfect day for a housewarming, meet-the-neighbors, barbecue sort of thing. Everyone I've met on our street so far has been incredibly nice, and Mrs. Gomez next door said we could use her barbecue pit."

"You're right, Aunty Jacq, I hate this idea," I said, rolling my eyes and sitting down on a stool in front of the breakfast bar. It was one of my favorite parts of the new house. Living off base sure had its perks.

Aunty Jacq gave me a wink and placed a small plate of short-breads in front of me with a glass of milk. I winked back.

"Actually, that wasn't exactly the idea we'd hoped you'd like," Mom said.

"*You* hoped she'd like," Aunty Jacq corrected her.

"Right."

"So what's the idea?" I asked, not even looking up. Aunty Jacq's shortbreads were amazing. They were still warm, perfect for dipping into the cold milk.

"I know how long you've waited to have a pet . . ."

I jolted up from my buttery bliss.

". . . and I thought that moving to Frederick, to this house, was finally the right time for it."

"Oh, Mom! Yes! I agree! A dog! And I'll really take care of it. I'll be completely responsible. I'll take it out for walks and feed it and train it and everything. I promise." I jumped off the chair and continued to dream big and talk to myself. "I bet I could even find some doggy dress patterns online and make it some seriously cute skull sweaters for the winter."

"Rayna, hold on a second," Mom said.

I looked up at her expectantly, excited to finally, *finally* have the dog I'd been dreaming about ever since Mom went off to basic training when I was five. I glanced at Aunty Jacq, who looked concerned and began furiously wiping down the counters.

"Rayna," Mom said. "Sit back down a sec. I'll be right back."

I plopped down onto a stool and watched Mom go out to the garage. I couldn't believe this was finally happening.

A few minutes later, she returned holding a big, clear plastic box without a lid and set it next to me on the counter.

"What's this?" I asked, confused.

Instead of the tail-wagging bundle of joy I wanted, or even the consolation prize of a cat, inside sat a balled up, spiky . . . hedgehog.

"Rayna," Mom said. "Meet Spike."

6

An hour later, I sat fuming in the car. I was beyond angry. Shocked. Mom sat next to me in the driver's seat, swaying to a song on the radio. Her dark ponytail bounced around without a care in the world. She had to have known how much I wanted a dog and how long I'd wanted one. She *had* to. And if that was true, it meant she just didn't care. It hurt, and I was angry, so angry.

"This song's an oldie but goodie, right?" she asked, turning up the volume.

I stared out the window, not looking at anything in particular.

"There's always one oldies radio station, no matter where you go. Isn't that cool?" she asked, looking over at me. "I saw some really cute hedgehog cages at the pet store earlier. I think you're going to love them. And the young man who works there was really helpful. His name is Justin. I'm sure he'll have you all set up in no time."

Silence.

"Rayna?"

Silence.

Mom sighed. "This is going to be great, really. I think you're going to love having Spike around. I didn't get any supplies earlier because I thought you'd enjoy picking them out. You can ask Justin as many questions as you want. He's an expert. And Spike will be living in your room, so I know you'll want to get a cage you like."

I'd had enough. I was a volcano . . . erupting . . . couldn't hold it in . . . lots of words. *Boom!* "No. I won't like it, Mom. I don't want a stupid hedgehog. Have I ever asked for a hedgehog? No. I have always asked for a dog. Always. You know what a dog is, right? Four legs. Barks. Wags tail. A REAL pet. And now we're going to a store to buy things for a creature I don't want. Why are we even doing this?"

"Rayna, first, calm down, and watch your tone, young lady."

I ignored her. "You never listen to me. Why can't we just

go back home, get the rodent who I'm sure is going to know instantly that I hate it, and return it back to the 'expert' at the store? Trade it in for a dog. Why can't we just—"

"Stop right there," Mom said, her tone sharp and serious, full of military precision. "A hedgehog is a good first pet. Having a dog is a big responsibility, and we are not prepared to take that on right now. We need to get the house settled first. Get the family settled. I still need to find us a dentist and get a library card," she said as she turned down a broader street, picking up speed. "Just because you want a dog doesn't mean you're ready to care for one."

Tears formed in the corners of my eyes. I was twelve years old, not a baby. I took a breath, trying to calm the fire inside me. "You just bought me a pet, didn't you? Because you thought I could take care of it, right? Why not just exchange it? I promise, I will take very good care of a dog."

"I'm sorry, Rayna, but they need owners who are at home much more than we are."

"You mean much more than YOU are."

Silence filled the car. Full of unspoken words all painted in army green.

Mom silently turned on her blinker, easing our Honda hatchback off the street and into a strip-mall parking lot. A sign above a store tucked into the mall's corner read HAPPY PETS, HAPPY PEOPLE. A dog, a cat, and a goldfish with giant googly eyes all sprang from the name.

My mom's face was pinched and pale. It was the expression she always wore when she was trying not to show she was sad or hurt. But right then, I didn't care if she was hurt. I'd spoken the truth.

She parked near the store entrance, turned off the car, and took a breath. "Rayna, I know you would like a dog, but right now, today, that's not going to happen. If you take good care of this hedgehog, and show me that you can be responsible, I will consider getting you a dog next year." And with that, she opened her car door and got out. Before closing it, she looked back inside. "You coming in? Or am I picking out Spike's stuff for you?"

7

The first thing I noticed walking through the pet store doors were the skulls. Cute little purple-and-white skulls—on a doggy sweater. Ouch. Salt in the wounds.

I looked down at my feet, watching the skulls I was wearing on my sneakers follow my mom deeper into the store. I tried hard to accept my fate, to remember that if I did this well, took care of the hedgehog, a real pet would eventually wag its tail at me someday.

As my mom greeted the store clerk up ahead, I braced myself. I needed to be polite and do this right. My mom would be watching my attitude, and there was one thing I knew: She might not have been getting me a dog right then and there, but she didn't lie. If Mom said, "Maybe next year," she meant it.

"Here she is," Mom said as I approached. "Rayna, meet Justin. He's the young expert I was telling you about. He knows everything about hedgehogs."

I looked up, prepared to give my courteous half smile. But my face froze. Before me was the tallest teenager I'd ever seen. I forgot all about puppies and hedgehogs. All I saw was tall. He wore skinny jeans and a fitted blue long-sleeved T-shirt, which made him look even taller. His fluffy hair waved in multiple directions, and his thick glasses reflected the overhead fluorescent lights. I came to, realizing he was smiling at me with a wide, sincere grin.

"Um . . . hi?" I said.

"Hi," Justin responded, looking at my mom and then back at me. "So you're the new owner of a hedgie."

"It looks that way," I confirmed, trying to focus on the task at hand.

"Spike's a great little hedgehog. Wanna start with houses? Then we can choose some food, a pouch, all things hedgie."

"Um. Sure."

"I'm going to leave you two to it," Mom said, grabbing her phone from her purse. "I'll be outside in the car making a couple of calls. You good, Rayna?"

I nodded.

"Okay, I'll be back in a few," she said, and headed toward the front of the store.

"I'm tall," Justin said when I looked back his way.

"What? I mean, yes. Sorry?"

"I'm really tall. I know. It's a lot to take in at first. I don't want you to feel bad for being surprised by my height. Or for staring a little bit. It's okay."

"Thanks," I said, not knowing the best way to respond.

"Sometimes it's better to just say what folks are thinking and get it out there."

"Makes sense. Um, curious. How tall are you?"

"I'm six foot, seven inches."

My brain resisted calculating that.

"Are you in college or something?"

"High school. I'm sixteen."

"Sixteen?!"

"Yeah."

"Is that tall for your age?"

"I don't know, maybe?"

"Does it hurt?" I asked, loosening up a little with a smirk.

"Ha! You've got spunk. Perfect for hedgie ownership."

I smiled. All the usual walls I'd built to shut people out seemed to have evaporated. I felt like I could tell Justin anything. "To tell you the truth, I didn't want a hedgehog."

"You didn't? Your mom seemed so excited about it. I thought you must be a huge fan."

"No. I really, really want a dog, you know? But my mom doesn't think I'm responsible enough."

"I get it. I love dogs, too. All animals actually. Someday I'm going to be a vet. Maybe even work with horses or big animals like elephants. I mean, they won't be that big to me," he said, throwing his head back and laughing a hearty laugh.

I couldn't help it. I laughed, too. All my stress about not getting a dog lightened a little. I was feeling better.

"Hedgehogs are actually super cool animals if you'll give them a chance," he said, coming out from behind the counter. "It takes time for them to trust you, though. They're kind of shy at first and don't make friends easily."

That sounded familiar.

"Let's go over to the hedgehog houses," he said, leading me down a long aisle with a low shelf holding different kinds of cages at its end. "This here is my favorite," he said, pointing to a black one. "It has two regular levels and one at the bottom that's covered so they can hide when they're feeling antisocial. There's plenty of room for them to climb around. You can even put in an exercise wheel on this one. Some hedgies dig them."

"Is it expensive? My mom didn't tell me what I could spend."

"Not really."

"Oh. Good. Okay. Sold, I think."

After setting the cage on the counter and grabbing a shopping basket, Justin took me from one side of the store to the other, showing me all kinds of toys and accessories that would be good for a hedgehog. Then we hit the food aisle, and I saw the packages of live worms.

"Hedgies love mealworms," Justin said, grabbing one from the shelf. "It's like their pizza or French fries, you know? Their junk food. Too much and they'll get fat, but it's great for training them—and getting them to like you."

I was totally digging the worms. How disgusting and cool!

Hedgies were turning out to be a little macabre, like me. The worms reminded me of Oogie Boogie in *The Nightmare Before Christmas*. Justin grabbed a few cans of a different food, and I followed him back to the front counter.

"Let's see, what else can I tell you? Oh yeah, hedgehogs are nocturnal, like little vampires," he said.

Perfect, I thought.

"They don't see very well, but they have a very sensitive nose. That's why they sometimes do their anointing."

"Anointing?"

"Yeah, it's weird, but smart. If they don't like how they smell, they'll lick their bodies until they smell like themselves again. And if they really like a new smell, they will find a way to mix their saliva with it and anoint their whole bodies with their new-smelling spit."

I couldn't help it. That cracked me up.

"So what all are we getting today?" Mom asked, surprising me with her presence. I suddenly stopped laughing and my shoulders tensed. I really didn't want my mom to know that I was warming to the hedgehog idea.

"I've got Rayna set up with all the essentials: a cage, a nice fake rock for Spike to hide under, a hedgie pouch to carry him around in when he's not in his cage, and food. Of course, you can always come back for more worms or whatever you need," Justin said.

"Great. Ring us up then, Justin. Thank you for helping Rayna today," Mom said, looking over at me and smiling.

My face was frozen. "Thanks, Mom," I said robotically.

She seemed satisfied, opening her purse and pulling out her credit card. I had to admit, Justin had been super cool and easy to hang around with. I hadn't laughed that much in a long time, and it felt good—even if my mom saw. Still, I needed to be careful and stick to the plan: grades, dog, no making friends. My mind started to drift back to Pensacola, back to my so-called friends ghosting me, back to just being another army brat kids liked to ignore.

"Oh, Rayna, one last thing," Justin said, pulling me from my thoughts and handing me the bag. "Don't forget to talk to your hedgie. Since they don't see well, they really use their ears to figure out their environment. Eventually, your hedgie will recognize your voice when you call it."

I nodded, giving him a small wave as we headed toward the front door.

On our way home, I was happy that my mom kept the oldies radio station on in the car. I turned up the volume as "Twist and Shout" rumbled out of the speakers so we wouldn't have to talk.

I watched my new town slip from block to block through the car window. Soon I'd have to really get to know my new pet, and I'd be lying if I said I wasn't just a tiny bit okay about it. No, Spike wasn't a puppy, but after hearing everything Justin had said about hedgehogs, I tried to be positive. Who knew? Maybe me and Spike would fall madly in love with each other, be friends for life. I doubted it, but it couldn't hurt to hope.

Could it?

8

HISSSSSS! Spike said, tightening himself into a ball. Our introductions were not going well. Any hopes that we'd be friends for life were quickly popping into nothingness.

I stood over the cranky creature, watching him hide in one of the corners of the plastic bin that I now had up on my desk. He was giving me spikes galore. How many times had I tried to pick him up and put him in his new house? Maybe ten? *Enough already!*

I sighed and sat down on my bed. My room was a mess, piled high with moving boxes. But at least I had my favorite things unpacked. I put the thrift-shop drafting table I used as a desk in front of the window where I would have the best light. My twin bed was covered in my favorite purple sheets and fuzzy black pillows. And my deep red nightstand held a white lamp and a stack of my favorite books. By the closet, my tall black mirror took up a whole corner of the room. *All mirrors should be black,* I thought, smiling.

I looked back at the new and very empty hedgehog cage next to my desk. My mom had given me a small table to put it on, and it actually fit in with my things pretty well. But that didn't mean Spike wanted to live in it. I understood how he felt. He'd been taken from the pet store and brought to a new place to stay. A place he didn't choose.

I decided to try again. "Hey, Spike. I know you probably don't want to be here. I mean, I get it. I really don't want to be here either. Or maybe I'm just scared to be here. Is that how you feel, too?" I slowly moved my hand down into the bin. "I won't hurt you. Ever. I'm not like that. All I want to do is put you into your new home so you don't have to stay in this plastic box. Is that okay?" I placed my hand near his body, lightly touching his quills.

Hufffff! Snort huff!!! Spike spat, running to another corner of the bin and rolling into a ball.

"Fine," I told the grumpy, quill-covered rodent. "Live in a plastic box for all I care." I sighed again, loudly—which sounded a lot like Spike—and stomped back over to my bed, plopping down. I had lost all patience. "Grrr!" I said, lying back onto my black fuzzy pillows. *Why didn't Mom just get me a dog?*

The smell of Aunty Jacq's veggie lasagna baking in the oven seeped into the room from the kitchen. *Mmmmm. Lasagna.* My muscles relaxed. But it would take at least another hour before dinner was ready. And there were moving boxes everywhere. "Well, Rayna Snow, looks like you've got more than enough to do."

I sat up and grabbed my headphones and phone from my backpack by the bed, turned on some of my favorite vintage emo music, and went to work.

First, I put Spike's plastic bin atop his new cage. At least he could get used to his new geography. Then I went straight for the boxes labeled SHOE LOVE stacked near the desk. From the top box, I pulled out a large piece of muslin with paint stains all over it. I smiled, unfolding it and laying it across the top of my desk.

Next, I took out my art supplies. Sorting through the items, I organized them by material and color. Old coffee cans held my paintbrushes and markers. Shoeboxes covered in different colors of construction paper held different tubes and bottles of acrylic paint. A big water jar for cleaning my brushes now sat at the ready. And sketch pads, stencils, and cans of sealant fit neatly in a pile under the desk.

Out of the last box, I pulled out an unfinished pair of Converse sneakers and placed them lovingly in the middle of the desk. Everything was exactly where it was supposed to be, ready and waiting for me to open up my paints and get to work.

I sat down and turned up my music. I opened my sketch pad and looked over the last drawing I'd made in Pensacola. It was of four Day of the Dead sugar skulls with different swirling designs on each one like in the *Coco* movie. *If I were from a Mexican family like in the movie*, I thought, *I'd have the biggest Day of the Dead altar ever. I'd put pictures of the friends Mom lost in Iraq. Nonna Laura and Nonno Olindo. And all the zias.*

I began adding some scalloped designs around the eyes of the skulls and decided to paint a few. At least a lot of Italian families like mine had All Souls' Day. It was also a day to remember people who had died. I let my imagination take over my paintbrush, and soon nothing mattered but my paints, the music, and the skeleton faces smiling at me. Nothing else existed: no unpacked boxes, no new house or town or school.

"Rayna!" Aunty Jacq yelled. I leapt, finding her standing right next to me, which scared me to death. I yanked the earphones from my ears. "Dinner's ready. Been calling you for ten minutes," she said.

"Sorry! Thanks, Aunty Jacq. I'll be right there." I dropped my paintbrush into the jar of water.

Aunty Jacq lingered in the doorway. "Your mom's being awful quiet out there. How did things go today at the pet store?"

I sighed. "Sorta okay. I'm really going to try with Spike. And she did say if I did a good job with him, next year could bring me a dog. But . . ." I hesitated. "I probably hurt her feelings."

"I see," she said.

"I didn't say anything that wasn't true. I just didn't say it nicely."

"Maybe you could make her some hot tea later?" Aunty Jacq asked.

I knew what that meant. Whenever we needed to say we were sorry, we always made a coffee or a tea or something to bring with it—something to share.

I nodded and followed her out toward the kitchen. But just before I left the room, I had a strange feeling, like someone was staring at me. I looked back toward the desk. Spike was peering at me quietly from inside the bin.

9

Saturday morning I dressed quickly. I was starving, even though I had eaten nearly my weight in lasagna the night before.

I checked on Spike in the bin. He was so confusing. Throughout the night, I'd heard him rustling around, but now he was just a spiky, silent, uninterested ball.

Justin had said he was nocturnal. He'd also said to talk to hedgehogs. Okay . . . fine.

"Hey, Spike. How are you doing? You definitely are a night owl, or I guess a night *hog?*"

Spike didn't move.

"So what should we talk about?"

Silence.

"I really don't have a lot to say today. I mean, I've got a lot on my mind. A bunch of neighbors are supposed to come to the house today. Terrible. And I have to text a boy. But I really don't want anything to do with people today.

"By the way, it's not your fault that you ended up with someone like me—you know, a dog person. Sorry about that. I promise I won't treat you badly, even if I didn't choose you myself."

I watched Spike's rapid breathing. He was in a deep sleep. I could have put my music on at top decibel, and he'd probably just lie there.

"I guess now would be a good time to tell you that I'm not mad at you or anything. I don't know if you can feel it when someone's mad? They say dogs can smell fear. Can hedgies smell twelve-year-olds feeling totally frustrated?"

I resisted trying to give him some pats.

"I'll be back later, okay?" I said, and bolted from my room.

Aunty Jacq was waiting for me in the kitchen, surrounded by the glorious smell of warm cranberries and wearing her favorite apron.

"Cranberry pecan pancakes?!" I asked, smiling. I couldn't help it. I *loved* this breakfast.

"Yep. Conosco i miei polli," Aunty Jacq said. "I know my chickens."

I grinned at her. Aunty Jacq had told me that was what my grandfather used to say. He'd immigrated to the US from eastern Italy. Knowing your chickens means you know your loved ones well, what they like, all their little tics and habits and favorite things.

I sat at the breakfast bar, grabbed a fork, and dove in to the crunch of pecans, the tartness of cranberries, the salty butter, and maple syrup. Heaven.

"I haven't seen that smile in a while," Aunty Jacq teased.

"Shhh . . ." I teased back. "Cranberry goodness happening."

"Mm-hmm. I hear you. But I want to give you a little encouragement to go with those cranberries."

I knew what was coming. She was about to talk to me *again* about Mom, so I cut her off before she could start in on me. "I apologized to Mom last night. I even brought her that chamomile lavender tea she likes."

"I know, Angel, and that was a very mature and thoughtful

thing for you to do. I just wanted to tell you that it may seem like your mom isn't paying attention to how you're feeling, but she really is trying to make this move easier on you—and me."

I sighed deeply, holding a bite of pancake on the fork midway to my mouth.

"Give her a chance to show you that, okay? Before you assume she doesn't care?" Aunty Jacq asked.

I wanted to roll my eyes, but I couldn't be upset with Aunty Jacq. She was so full of love and poured that love into all she made—her cooking, her art, her "chickens." She could be fierce and strong when needed—like the time we were in a car accident because a man had run a stop sign. He had gotten out of his car saying "women couldn't drive," and boy, she'd let him have it, telling him she had a child in the car, that the crash was his fault because he'd run the stop sign, and she'd make sure he was held responsible. A lot of Italian curse words that I didn't understand at the time were thrown about. She had fire in her, like me, but a lot of love, too.

Aunty Jacq looked at me expectantly. "Promise you'll give all this . . ." She waved her hands around, gesturing at the house, ". . . this new part of our story, a real go."

47

"Okay, Aunty Jacq," I said, looking her in the eyes. "I'll try."

"Good," she said. "Now where is that hair tie I had earlier. The humidity has my hair in a larger state of puff than usual." She felt around in her apron pocket and came up victorious. "Ha!" she said, then pulled her dark waves up into a jumble on top of her head.

"Oh, Aunty Jacq. I forgot to ask yesterday. Is it okay if I give my phone number to someone at school?"

"Who?" she asked curiously.

"His name is Nick Smallwood, and he's going to give me his social studies notes so I can catch up."

"Nick, huh? Cute? Nice? Responsible?"

I turned beet red.

"So he *is* cute, is he?" Aunty Jacq chuckled, but didn't torture me further. "I think that would be fine, Angel. I'll let your mom know."

Relief flooded my bones. "Thanks, Aunty Jacq. It's *just* for school."

"What's just for school?" my mom asked, coming in from the backyard covered in soil.

"What's with the dirt?" I asked.

48

"I asked you first," Mom said.

"Rayna would like to give her number to a cute boy at school," Aunty Jacq said, smiling wildly.

"Aunty Jacq!" I squeaked. "That's not—"

"It's okay, Angel. Don't worry. Kate, I told Rayna it was okay if she gave her number to Nick . . . What's his last name?"

"Smallwood," I said.

"I said she could give her number to this Nick Smallwood, so she can catch up on her social studies class," Aunty Jacq explained.

"I need to review the first unit," I said, getting up and taking my empty plate over to the sink to give it a rinse.

"Smallwood. That sounds familiar. Okay, you can give him your number, but give me his number, too, please."

"Thanks, Mom. I will," I said, drying my hands.

"Now that you're done eating, why don't you put some proper shoes on. I'm going to need some help setting up for the barbecue today."

Right . . . the barbecue. The cranberries had made me briefly forget my fate. I had hoped Mom had decided a backyard event would be too much work when we were still unpacking, but nope. I'd have to spend the day dealing with strangers.

"Don't get twisted up about it," Mom said. "It will be fun! I've almost got all the dead branches moved out of the way out back, and I could use your help setting up some chairs."

"Sure, Mom. I'll help."

Aunty Jacq looked up from filling a container with leftover pecans. She beamed at me with pride and gave me a thumbs-up.

"I hate it, but I'll help," I said, crossing my arms.

Aunty Jacq threw her hands up to the ceiling.

"You know, Jacq, this backyard is really in good shape," Mom said. "I could probably have the beds ready to plant a garden as early as spring."

The pit of my stomach turned sour. I didn't want to hear about gardens. I never understood the point of them, especially when we had to just leave them behind anyway. Once, we tilled up nearly a whole backyard so Mom could grow tomato plants. She'd said she'd use the tomatoes to make sauce. And then we'd had to move.

But gardening was Mom's hobby, like shoe painting was mine and cooking was Aunty Jacq's. Mom liked being in nature when she had free time, since she spent her workdays and missions writing and analyzing code on high-tech computers. So at home, Mom was Sergeant First Class of Backyard Gardening, though knowing the army, we'd probably end up with disappointing dirt all over again.

Soon Mom and Aunty Jacq were talking about all the veggies that could be grown in Maryland. With them distracted, I ever so slowly slipped out of the kitchen and back to my room. I had to face another uncomfortable fate anyway. I had to text Nick.

10

The words *Hi Nick. It's me, Rayna* glowed up at me from my phone screen, mocking me.

I sat at my desk, waiting for a response. When ten minutes passed and I'd heard nothing, I started to wonder. *Did I get the number right?* I looked again at the torn piece of paper Nick had given me and felt like an idiot, waiting on some boy to text me back. Maybe I could catch up on my own. I'd done it before. All I'd need was some—

Hey Rayna

I nearly jumped out of my skin, dropping the phone onto the desk. *He responded! Wait, why am I excited?* I felt ridiculous. I was only texting for the As. I just had to remember that. Those lovely, wonderful, spiky As. *Be cool, Rayna. Just be cool.*

> Obvs my mom said it was ok to give u my number

I can see that

. . .

> You said we could meet?

. . .

Are you serious right now? Just text me back. Let's get this over with.

Sorry my dad called me

> No worries.

Then thought: *Yep, I'm lying.*

I'm free Monday

Can you meet after school?

> I take the bus home

K?

> So I have to get on the bus after school

That's usually how it works

That's actually funny.

> I mean

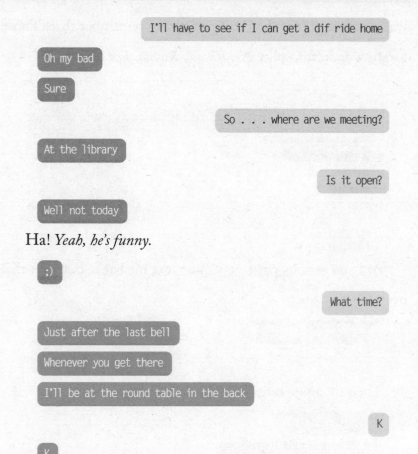

I'll have to see if I can get a dif ride home

Oh my bad

Sure

So . . . where are we meeting?

At the library

Is it open?

Well not today

Ha! *Yeah, he's funny.*

;)

What time?

Just after the last bell

Whenever you get there

I'll be at the round table in the back

K

K

I set the phone down on my desk. *That wasn't terrible.* Even if butterflies were on a rampage in my belly. *Why does my new study buddy have to be cute?* I tried to think of my grades, not his turquoise eyes and long hair . . . *Stop already!*

To distract myself, I picked up the sneakers I'd been working on the night before. The base color of paint that I'd put along the back heels was almost dry. I could sketch on the top design later that afternoon.

Suddenly, I heard a rustling. I'd nearly forgotten I was a pet owner! I looked at Spike inside the bin. Spike looked back. *Is he trying to be brave like me? Make a sort-of friend?* I rose slowly from my desk, moved the bin over to my desk, and opened the cage to the hedgehog house.

"It's all right, Spike. I just want to put you in your new home, okay?"

Spike stared at me as I reached my hand slowly into the bin, and with a little coaxing, I was able to scoot one hand up underneath him.

All of a sudden, Spike came alive! The hedgie's nose twitched and sniffed my hand all over, first my palm, then my fingers. I placed my other hand underneath him as well and lifted him out, watching him sniff and sniff, as if he was making sure not to miss a spot. When Spike had sniffed every crevice he could find and seemed satisfied, I very tenderly placed him down into the hedgehog house. I couldn't help but smile from ear to ear. We'd both been brave. Victory.

11

The Saturday-afternoon sun had begun to set over Frederick, shining a sideways light on our new backyard. And what I saw there was terrible. A capital-*T* kind of Terrible. There were people everywhere, smiling and chatting and acting like meeting us was the greatest thing ever. I hated every second of it. All I wanted to do was retreat to my room and paint or see what Spike was up to, but Mom had made it very clear that escape wasn't an option.

From my folding chair near the fence, all the chatting and eating seemed so fake and meaningless. To me, they could have been aliens disguised as humans, desperate for acceptance at backyard barbecues. I giggled under my breath. Aliens might make a good design for a pair of painted Converse. I pulled the sleeves of my favorite black-and-white hoodie down over my hands so the coldness of my grape soda wouldn't freeze my fingers. I planned to stay under the radar for the next hour, then forget it all even happened. No such luck. My mom was headed straight toward me holding a green piece of paper followed by a trio of aliens.

"Rayna, this is our neighbor Mr. Jacobson. He also used to work at the base, but he's retired now. He tells me that the local Army National Guard is teaming up with the VFA to put on a pet talent show. It's to benefit retired K9s on National K9 Veterans Day.

"I was just telling Mr. Jacobson all about Spike. Isn't this amazing timing, Rayna? You and Spike could join the contest, meet folks, and do some good for the local VFW."

I wasn't really listening, but I stood up and gave Mr. Jacobson a polite smile.

"Look at the flyer. Isn't it sweet?" Mom asked, handing me the paper, which was decorated with an image of a soldier kneeling down by a large German shepherd. It read:

JOIN US

MARCH 13
FOR OUR FIRST EVER
COMMUNITY PET TALENT SHOW
BENEFITING OUR
RETIRED FOUR-LEGGED WARRIORS

HELP US HONOR
THE FAITHFULNESS AND COURAGE
OF OUR K9 MILITARY VETS

"Please, call me Dan," the man said. "It's nice to meet you, Rayna. We would be honored to have you join us. I know you and Spike are brand-new buddies, but you'll have plenty of time to discover his new talents before next spring."

"So you want me to sign up for a contest that helps *dogs?*" I asked my mother incredulously. *How can she even think I'd be up for this?*

"Yes, ma'am, I do," Mom said. I knew better than to argue. She had that look on her face I knew all too well. This here event would be nonnegotiable.

"There's some prize money in it for the entrants, too," Dan said excitedly—like that mattered to me.

Courteous half smile. "Thank you, Mr. Jac—I mean, Dan," I said, holding the paper in one hand and my grape soda in the other.

"Kate, have you met your neighbors from across the street yet?" Dan asked.

"Not yet," Mom said. She gave me a be-on-your-best-behavior look and followed Dan across the yard.

Finally. I was out of there. I turned and rushed across the backyard, through the back door, and into the kitchen. There I could escape the terrible aliens and their silly contests. I headed straight to the refrigerator and opened the door.

It wasn't even that hot outside, but having the fresh, cool air of the refrigerator flow over my face gave me the perfect, quiet moment to get ahold of myself.

A beautiful cheesecake sat on the middle shelf inside. I was done with the alien crowd, but if Aunty Jacq planned to serve that today . . . well, I'd make an exception. Plus, I had promised Aunty Jacq that very morning that I'd give Mom a chance. I grabbed another grape soda and shut the door.

When I turned around, I saw something that made me jump.

Three pairs of eyes were watching me from the other side of the small kitchen island. Creepy. At least I recognized them. Marcie and the blue-and-green backpack boys.

"So are you going to enter the pet talent show?"

"Kevin, geez. Maybe introduce yourself first?" Marcie said, then turned to me. "I'm not sure if you remember me from yesterday. I'm Marcie. We have science together? I live in the yellow-and-white house across the street. And these two *rude* people are Kevin and Matt Stone. They're in sixth grade and live in the house with the giant oak tree out front. Sorry to sneak up on you. No one our age has moved to Camden Lane before."

"Hi," said Kevin.

"Hi," said Matt.

"Uh, hi," I said. I knew I should probably ask them about themselves or school or something—be a good host and try to make polite conversation—but I didn't know what to say that wouldn't sound fake. And the longer I was quiet, the faster my heart raced.

"So are you going to enter the contest?" Kevin asked.

"What contest?" I replied, pretending I didn't know what he meant.

"This one," Matt said, holding up the green flyer, resting on the kitchen island.

"Oh, that," I said. "I don't know. My mom gave me the—"

"What kind of pet do you have?" Kevin asked.

"Let her answer the first question," Marcie instructed. All three of them looked at me, waiting for an answer.

"My mom just gave me the flyer. And I . . . uh . . . just got a pet, but I don't think he's the trainable kind." *Why, why am I telling them this?*

"It's a snake, huh?" Matt asked.

"No, not a sna—"

"Lizard?" Kevin asked.

"No, a—"

"Fish?" Matt asked.

"No!" I said, exasperated. "Um . . . sorry. I mean, no. It's a—"

"We have a parrot," Kevin said, "an African gray one. We're going to teach her to say a line from a movie. Gayle already knows some phrases, but we're thinking she should say 'To infinity and beyond!' like in *Toy Story*."

"I thought we nixed that one," Matt said, looking at his

brother like he was the most annoying animal on the planet. "Too many vowels."

"No, *you* wanted to nix it. I say it's still in the running," Kevin said.

"They do this," Marcie said, giving me a knowing look. "I have a golden retriever who is good at catching things. But that's kind of boring. It's for a good cause, though, right? All those K9 dogs are so brave."

"Marcie, you've got it easy," Matt said. "Daisy's smart. Gayle is kinda old and hasn't learned to say anything new in a long time."

"Just 'cause Gayle is thirty doesn't mean she can't still learn," Marcie countered.

"Thirty?!" I shrieked.

"Yeah. Parrots can live up to forty years in captivity," Kevin explained. "My dad's had Gayle since he was our age." He pointed to the drink in my hand. "You got any more of that grape soda?"

"Sure," I said, opening the fridge again and grabbing a can for him.

Marcie chuckled. "There's this crazy picture of us. I'll have to show it to you. It's me, Matt, and Kevin in matching space pajamas, and Gayle is sitting on Matt's shoulder. She almost feels like an aunt or something."

Great. They've known each other since they were babies. I couldn't help it. Jealousy was taking over. I wanted out of the kitchen. *No friends,* I told myself. *You don't need them.*

"That's true, but she really is smart," Kevin said.

"Listen, guys," Marcie said, "we just have to treat this like a mission at Space Camp."

The trio began to relive their summer pretending to be astronauts, and I realized that this was my chance to leave without them noticing. I slowly backed out of the kitchen—my second kitchen escape of the day—and headed for the front porch.

Outside, I took a deep, soothing breath. Finally, I was alone.

"Hey," a voice said.

12

I whirled around on the porch to find the girl from the bus who'd been wearing the neon-pink T-shirt. She sat cross-legged on the porch by the door, looking at a bona fide smartphone.

"Wilma Ryan," she said, gesturing to herself.

"Um, Rayna Snow," I said.

Wilma's straight, dark blonde hair was pulled up in a tight ponytail atop her head. She wore a ton of eyeliner—AND she had a tiny silver stud in her nose. *Isn't she too young for that?*

"Can't help but stare at the nose ring, right?" she asked, not even looking up from her phone.

"Oh. I'm so sorry. Not really. I mean, not that I'm not really sorry. I mean, yes, I noticed it. But that's not what I was, um, thinking about. I was surprised. But not by the ring. I thought I was alone. Not that my mom would let me be today." I could feel the heat rising in my chest.

Wilma turned off her cell phone and gave me her full attention. Now I noticed that her eyeliner led to two blue dots she'd painted on the outside of her eyes. I would have told her it looked cool, but I was too mad.

"I mean, seriously, we *just* moved here. And already she's having a barbecue even though she knows I didn't want to!"

Wilma continued to listen.

"My mom's in the army, which means we might have to pack up and leave at any moment. Does she really have to act like we'll be here for good? That's ridiculous, right? I just don't get it." I could hear my voice getting louder, but I couldn't stop myself. "And now she's forcing me to enter this stupid pet talent show!"

"That's tough," Wilma said.

Relief spread over me when Wilma said that. It *was* tough. And I was so tired of it. I plopped down on the porch next to her like I'd known her forever. "Is it really TOO MUCH to ask to just be left alone this time? Let me sit in my room and worry about my grades? And, and . . . you know what else? She seriously lost all reason yesterday and got me this antisocial, moody, worm-eating hedgehog."

Wilma's eyebrows shot up. "Hedgehog?"

"Yeah, can you believe it? Aunty Jacq says give it a go, give her a break, give him a—"

"Seriously, you own a hedgehog?" Wilma repeated.

"Yeah," I said.

"I want to see."

What? Wait. My room is, like . . . private. But Wilma seems cool . . . I shook my head. Still, I was too frustrated to argue, and heard myself say, "Sure."

Wilma followed me back into the house, through the entryway, down the short hall, and into my room.

"Wow, you painted all these?" Wilma asked, pointing at my custom Converse lining the wall.

I nodded.

"They're amazing. How many pairs do you have?"

"I think twenty-two?" I said. The anger I'd been feeling just minutes before began to slowly drip away. I was back in my happy place, surrounded by my paints, and Wilma seemed truly interested. But I could still feel an icy spot in my chest—the one warning me that this was *not* how you avoid making friends.

"Hey there," Wilma said to Spike as she peered into his cage, a small grin forming across her face. She looked my age—even with the nose ring.

"Are you in seventh grade?" I asked.

"Yeah. You?"

"Yeah."

"What's his name?"

"Spike."

"A little cliché but still cool," Wilma said, chuckling. She reached down into the cage, where Spike was sitting on the lower level.

"He's really antisocial. He may not let you—"

"There's a little guy," Wilma said, putting her hand underneath Spike and pulling him up and out of the cage. I couldn't believe it. Why didn't Spike hiss and snort and run off? She looked at him more closely at eye level and then carefully placed him back into his cage and closed the top. "I've always wanted a pet, but my dad is super allergic to just about everything. So, I have other hobbies."

I nodded again. Everything felt surreal. The afternoon was turning to evening, and the sideways light warmed parts of the room. Wilma leaned over my work-in-progress Converse on the desk and took a good look. The piece of paper with Nick's number caught her eye.

"Nick Smallwood, huh?" she asked, lifting her eyebrows again. "He's cute."

I turned beet red but said nothing. I was NOT about to go there. Besides, even though Wilma seemed really laid-back and cool and Spike seemed to like her, the truth was I really didn't know her. I'd said too much about my life already.

"I probably should find my mom or my aunt," I said. "I'm supposed to be helping, but, well . . . I guess I—"

"Needed a break?" Wilma asked.

"Yeah," I said. "But if I stay gone too long, I know I'll get an earful later."

"Sure. I need to head back to my house anyway. My dad gets home soon."

"He didn't come?"

"No, he's out with Kentucky."

I looked at Wilma quizzically.

"That's what I call his girlfriend. She's from Kentucky. Has this crazy accent," Wilma said, heading to my door.

"Oh," I said, frozen like a statue in the middle of my room.

"Bye, Spike," Wilma said over her shoulder as she headed out. "And nice to meet you, Rayna, Owner of Cool Hedgehog."

"You too," I said, but my words met empty space. Wilma had already left the room.

13

Sunday came and went, and so had my mom. Just as I had suspected, the army didn't wait long to ship her off. They'd called Saturday night, telling her she was needed out on the West Coast in a joint army-navy exercise. The time she had off for our move was officially over. I couldn't help but feel like a timer had been set, counting down until they'd move us again. Any day the timer would go *ding* and that would be it.

I went to school Monday fully prepared to fend off unwanted attention and conversation from everyone I'd met at the barbecue. I wore black from head to toe and my fiercest pair of Converse with their red-eyed, fiery skulls. I'd pulled my black hoodie down over my face on the bus and avoided as much eye contact as I could.

Nick gave me a quick "hey" in Mr. Toliver's class, but that was all. I was glad because looking at Nick too long made my head feel like it was going to pop, and I needed to focus on listening and taking notes. I was dreading our afternoon study session. But it was too important. I really needed help catching up.

When lunch came, I ate by myself in the corner of the cafeteria. It was beautiful. Things were working out great. Maybe the barbecue was a fluke, and Matt, Kevin, and Marcie had already forgotten about the new girl on the street. I hoped that I could avoid everyone, every day . . . forever—but then, science class happened.

Marcie plopped down in the seat beside me. "Hi, Rayna," she said.

"Hey." I wondered if she was going to stay there. We did have assigned seats, and that wasn't hers. We sat next to one another silently for a second, not saying anything. Marcie seemed totally okay with that. I looked at the clock on the wall. There were three more minutes till the bell rang.

"Thanks for inviting us over on Saturday," she finally said.

I didn't, I thought back.

Marcie turned and looked at me with complete kindness. "I'm sorry that me, Kevin, and Matt nerded out on you. We've known each other forever, and our inside jokes can get kinda . . . boring, but the guys were really looking forward to meeting you. It's so cool to have a new person on our street, you know?"

I didn't. "No worries," I said, feeling guilty that I wanted her to go back to her seat. She truly seemed super nice.

"Did you meet Wilma? I thought I saw her hanging around."

"Yeah."

"Oh, good! Well, you've met us all then. Okay, I'm going to go back to my seat. We're doing gases today. I'm so excited!" Her eyes lit up like fireworks, and she headed back to her seat.

Soon, science class turned into math class, which turned into my last class of the day, language arts. I'd studied hard for the quiz we were having, and when the teacher handed back our papers just before the bell rang, I was happy to find a bright, spiky A staring up at me!

Now all I had to do was make it through my study session, meet up with Aunty Jacq, who'd agreed to drive me home, and do it all again the next day. *I can do this,* I thought. *Avoid people, study, huzzah!*

I walked quickly to my locker, threw the books I didn't need inside, and slammed the door shut. I was Done for the day with a capital *D.* But the day wasn't done with me. I sighed and headed toward the library to meet Nick.

Bzzzz. My phone went off. I pulled it out of my backpack to see a message from Nick, telling me that he had to pick up something from the office but would only be a couple of minutes late. *Good,* I thought. If I hurried, I wouldn't have to make an awkward entrance.

Not even a minute later, I burst through the library doors and was met with a bitter glare from the librarian sitting at the library desk.

"Sorry," I whispered. A round table sat in the back corner. I headed over, plunked down, and pulled out my social studies book, spiral notebook, and pen. I laid them out all neatly in front of me. *Good, okay, good. I'm ready.*

When I looked up, Nick's megawatt smile warmed me from across the room. He waved and put his finger up, to let me know to hold on a sec while he spoke with the librarian. They seemed chummy. My heart beat . . . a lot. *Come on, Rayna, don't be silly.*

You're not here to focus on an amazing smile. Stick to the subject. SOCIAL STUDIES. I took a deep breath.

He finally made it to the table and sat down. "Thanks so much for being cool about the time."

"Sure," I said, noticing every detail about him: from his long brown braid that was only just beginning to show some wear from the day, to the green T-shirt that made his eyes even more turquoise, to his easy nature.

"I didn't have a chance to tell you earlier today, but I really dig those mad skulls on your sneaks."

"Oh, um, thanks."

"They're a little more vicious than the ones you wore Friday, right?"

He noticed both pairs? I nodded, unable to respond.

"Cool. Okay, Unit One. You're actually really lucky."

Lucky? Blank stare.

"I mean, you really haven't missed too much," he said.

"Oh, right. Okay." I tried to seem cool. Chill. Not too friendly, not too distant. But I could feel all my walls shooting up tall around me.

Nick slid a set of stapled pages across the table to me. It was a copy of his handwritten notes. "Ms. Abbot in the office made a copy for you."

"Thanks," I said, feeling my hands going clammy. *Can he tell that I'm nervous? Why am I nervous?* I felt so stupid. "You know, I could probably just look at your notes and read the chapters at home." I put his notes in my bag and began gathering my things. "I mean. You don't have to show me stuff if you don't want to."

Nick touched my arm. His hand was warm and gentle, but firm. "Hold on there. It's totally cool, Rayna, really. How about I show you which chapters are the most important to help you get started, and we'll leave it at that?"

His hand was still on my arm. I felt zingy—like a buzz was growing in my ears. "I, uh, um, sure," I said.

"Cool. Okay," he said, taking his hand back. "The most important thing is to read chapters one and two. There's usually a question from there on every quiz."

"Thanks," I said.

"You know, I think we have something in common. You mentioned the other day that your mom was in the army?"

"Yeah, Sergeant First Class. Works in cybersecurity."

"Wow, that's cool! My dad was in the army. He retired last year, though. Now he's a civilian and works for the VFW."

"He retired? How old is he?"

"Oh, it's not like that. He's only forty-one. He just decided he was done being *in* the army and let his time run out. They don't really call it retiring, but it's not quitting either. It's like letting a contract run out?"

I hadn't known that choosing anything after joining was possible.

"And he picked here for you to live?" I asked.

"Yeah, Frederick's home for us! It was kind of hard on my mom before, with all the moving. He could be gone a lot. But he really loves working with vets and the VFW. He feels like he's giving back, you know?"

A dark, oozing feeling began to bubble up around my ears. I looked at Nick. Cute Nick. Nice Nick. And hated his guts. It wasn't fair. It just wasn't. From the way my mom talked, she'd never leave the army.

Then I remembered the green flyer. "Does he work for the same VFW that's sponsoring the pet talent show for K9 Veterans Day?" I asked, glaring.

"Yes! You know it? I came up with the idea. I love the K9s."
Nick was beaming. "But sometimes they need special care after
being in war zones, and vets don't always have the money for it.
Can't leave our four-legged brothers like that. Anyway, I was training Mr. Unega this summer and he was getting really good at some
tricks and I thought, let's do a show in the park and raise money."

"Mr. Unega?" I asked.

"That's my dog. He's a Jack Russell. They're the coolest. We
call him Mr. Unega because when he was a pup he was completely white. *Unega* means *white* in Cherokee. I'm Cherokee, by
the way," he said. "Mr. Unega's got some other colors in his coat
now, though, but the name stuck."

The dark, gooey, oily, terrible ooze grew bigger and bigger,
taking over everything inside me. *He gets to stay in a town AND
he has a dog*? I thought. I felt stupid and embarrassed and jealous,
all at the same time.

"I gotta go." I stood, trying not to let Nick see my pinched face.

"Hey, Rayna, you okay?"

"I'm sorry, I just can't . . ."

"Is it something I said? Wait . . ." he said, his tone sobering.
"Do you have issues with Indians or something?"

"What?" My eyes went wide in shock.

"I mean, you haven't seemed too happy to talk with me ever since Mr. Toliver asked me to help on Friday. I thought maybe you were just shy or something, but . . ." Nick glanced around the room. Then he looked right at me. The once-warm turquoise eyes now had a sad, angry look in them—like a hurt that came from somewhere deep inside him.

"Oh no. I'm sorry, Nick. Not at all. I'm not judging. I just . . . I can't explain," I said, not knowing how to even begin to apologize properly.

"Not judging," he said, unbelieving.

I had no idea what to do or say. Besides, he was jumping to conclusions and calling me a racist? "Well, what about you?" I asked. "You don't know me. Yet you're accusing me of some serious stuff. You think I'm judgmental?" I began to blurt things I didn't mean. "And . . . and . . . you act like I don't know how to even read a history book. Geez. Like I'm some dumb girl. I didn't even want your help."

"You're right. I don't know you," he said leaning back and crossing his arms.

And with that, I grabbed my bag and bolted from the library

as fast as I could. The hallway on the other side of the door felt like it was closing in on me. *This stupid school. This stupid, stupid school.* The orange-and-purple decorations loomed over me as I ran down the hall out the front entrance to the school's wide steps. *Please, Aunty Jacq. Please be here already.*

14

Halloween had definitely arrived at FMS. It was Friday, and the extravaganza was that night. I had a feeling that by lunchtime, teachers would give up trying to teach us anything. All anyone wanted to do was eat candy, have fun, and show off their craziest costumes. Some of them were spectacular, but costumes weren't my thing. Instead, I wore what I did every Halloween: head-to-toe pieces covered with Jack the Pumpkin King and my black, oversize hoodie with Jack's dog, Zero, on the back.

I was done with the quiz Mr. Tolliver had given us, so I sat staring at the back of Nick's denim jacket. It had been two weeks since he'd spoken to me. I couldn't help but notice that over the past few weeks, he'd seemed a little less cheery as a person. He'd stopped speaking up in class, and for someone like him, that was noticeable. He was just . . . off. I wanted to ask him about it, but I knew he didn't want to talk to me. And why would he? I had acted so horribly to him. If I had just told him what was going on, that there was no way I had any issues with him being Cherokee, that I had been upset, mostly with my mom, maybe we'd be cool now. But I hadn't. Instead, I'd been a jerk, and now we were where we were.

I looked away from Nick's jacket and played with my Pumpkin King bracelet, telling myself it didn't matter, even if the pit of my stomach felt like it was turning to stone. Marcie, Matt, and Kevin had been polite, but they weren't really talking to me or asking me to hang out. I barely saw Wilma. And I hadn't made an effort to get to know anyone else. The year was turning out exactly how it should. I hadn't wanted friends anyway, right?

I tried not to think about it and stared out the window. *Think positive thoughts,* I told myself. Not everything was awful. Things at home with my mom had smoothed over, or at least felt more normal. Mom called every night from San Diego. She said she'd be gone only another week or so. But who knew? It was okay. Or I was just used to it. And Aunty Jacq had finally set up a space for herself to do some painting. We'd become painting buddies after dinner, showing each other our work before bed. Even Spike seemed to be warming up to the place, and we had a pretty good routine.

Each morning, I'd clean out the straw full of poo from his cage. Yep. Hedgehogs were good at something after all. I'd put a few veggie pieces in his bowl with some hedgehog pellets, refill his water container, and say my hellos while he dozed.

After school, I'd pick him up and let the little quillball smell my hands. I'd reward him with a worm or two, which was totally gross but hilarious. Then I'd take him over to my bed and let him wander around on its covers for a little while. I still had no idea what I could train my hedgie to do for the contest. He seemed to be his own little man. I thought about just making him a cool outfit and calling him a hedgie supermodel, but Mom said that was *not* a talent. At night Spike would run on his wheel.

The bell rang, bringing me back to the classroom. I watched Nick get up from his seat and file out with everyone else. As usual, I waited for the room to clear, then grabbed my backpack and headed out.

Outside in the hallway, Nick was talking with Wilma. As I neared them, I heard Wilma say, "She didn't seem that way to me."

Are they talking about me? I wondered.

They both glanced in my direction, then lowered their voices. *Oh god, what if he told her about the library?* Wilma had been so cool to me at the barbecue, but if Nick had told her what he thought I was like, she probably hated me, too. I reminded myself that I didn't care. That this time around, I shouldn't care.

It still sucked.

Is this why everyone is leaving me alone? Not because I'm doing a good job keeping my distance, but because everyone thinks I'm a racist? This was not okay, but I didn't know how to fix it. As tears formed in my eyes, I quickly headed down the hall to my next class. When I got there, I grabbed my phone out of my bag and texted Aunty Jacq.

AJ, can u pick me up today?

Let me check

. . .

Sure

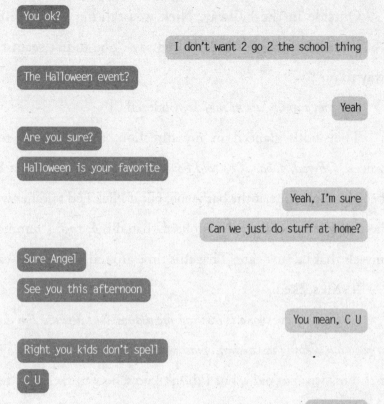

You ok?

I don't want 2 go 2 the school thing

The Halloween event?

Yeah

Are you sure?

Halloween is your favorite

Yeah, I'm sure

Can we just do stuff at home?

Sure Angel

See you this afternoon

You mean, C U

Right you kids don't spell

C U

Thx AJ ☺

15

It felt so good to be curled up on the couch in the living room watching one of the best movies of all time: *Coco*. I'd put on my favorite movie-watching outfit: soft skull-and-crossbones sweatpants and a matching hoodie. I quietly sang along with the film, trying to forget all my worries.

Aunty Jacq had really outdone herself. She'd put a whole tray of junk food and candy out, stocked the fridge with as much grape soda as I wanted, and made mini grilled cheese sandwiches for dinner. Plus, there hadn't been many trick-or-treaters at the door, so I sat next to a giant bowl of candy like a dragon with its hoard.

Spike had also joined our Halloween movie night. He'd really taken to his cozy carrying pouch the past few days and seemed to love it. I had to admit, it looked pretty snuggly. Every once in a while, Spike would leap out of the bag and run around the couch, sniffing Aunty Jacq's feet, then my feet, before diving back into his pouch.

I smiled down at the wiggly guy as he burrowed for some imaginary treat inside the bag. I was glad I'd listened to Aunty Jacq and given Spike a chance. I was still working on giving Mom one, but after the army called her away, it was nice having Spike to take care of. I pulled his pouch into my lap. Mom had said she would probably be back for Thanksgiving, but I knew it wasn't a guarantee. I had no idea exactly where she was, only that they'd sent her off from San Diego. I never did. Sometimes she'd tell us when she got back, but sometimes it just stayed a mystery. I knew she'd been to Hong Kong and Singapore last time, which sounded cool. I tried to imagine my mom in places across the world that were nothing like home. Sometimes, I'd look up the cities she went to online—even dream about being there with her, having our own adventure. But all I could ever really do was hope that she was safe. I might not have a Day of the Dead altar for everyone who had left us like Miguel's family in *Coco*, but I didn't want to add my mom to the list of people who'd "gone to the great beyond."

I looked over at Aunty Jacq, who'd drifted off during the movie. Her little plate of treats sat half eaten in front of her. She must have been really tired. In a couple of days, it would be time for our own traditions to remember those who had passed. Every November second—All Souls' Day—Aunty Jacq made a big Italian meal like her mom, my nonna, used to make, and she always pulled out all the old picture albums for us to look at.

My grandparents, Nonna and Nonno, had both passed away when I was a baby, when my mom was only eighteen and Aunty Jacq twenty-two. I didn't have any memories of them, but it still felt like I knew them anyway. Aunty Jacq told me stories about how they had loved to sail together before moving to the US. There were all kinds of pictures of them on sailboats in the Adriatic Sea. There were also lots of pictures of them eating around tables with friends even my mom and Aunty Jacq didn't know. They always looked super in love in their pictures. I hoped to have that someday, like the old couple in the movie *Up*. The kind of romance where your person was your very best friend—someone who really got you, let you be you, and loved who you were. I realized that Mom and Aunty Jacq didn't have anyone like that. Just each other. *Would that ever happen? Would Aunty Jacq ever find her person and move away?*

As the credits began to roll for *Coco*, Aunty Jacq stirred at the other end of the couch. "Hey, Angel, how are you holding up over there?"

"I'm good," I said. "What should we watch next: *Hotel Transylvania* or *Beetlejuice*?"

"*Beetlejuice*. Or how about *The Addams Family*? I love that one."

"For you, Aunty Jacq, let's do *Addams*." I smiled, grabbing the remote and scrolling over to our saved movies.

"You know, I wouldn't be a good aunty if I didn't ask you about school. How's it going so far?"

"It's just . . ." I started, setting the remote down on the edge of the couch. "Some of the kids in my classes may think I'm not a nice person."

"Why would they think that?" Aunty Jacq asked.

I hesitated. I kind of wanted to tell Aunty Jacq what happened with Nick, but I knew she would just encourage me to talk to him and Wilma and clear the air, and I wasn't ready to do that.

"It's just a feeling," I said.

"Mm-hmm," she said, giving me a little bit of side-eye, unbelieving. "If you say so."

I knew she wasn't buying it.

"It's nothing, really. And I promise I'll talk to you about it if I need to," I said, choosing the movie on the screen and changing the subject. "Aunty Jacq, how did Nonna Laura and Nonno Olindo pass away again?"

"You are such a cute, incredibly morbid, angel niece, so I'll let you off the hook about school . . . for now," she said, smiling. "I usually tell all those stories on November second."

"I know, but I'd like to hear about them tonight."

Aunty Jacq sat up and filled her snack plate with a few more treats and began her storytelling. "Nonno Olindo loved to build things and loved having his family near. Leaving Italy for the US was difficult, but he found work as an architect in Boston, Massachusetts, where a cousin was living—we Italians tend to follow our cousins. Anyway, Nonna Laura went with him to Boston, and they built a home in the suburbs back in the nineties. They loved going to Little Italy in the North End so they could be around other Italians. Now, Nonna Laura wasn't only Italian. Your great-grandfather, her father, was English, and his last name was Snow. So when they came to the US, Nonno Olindo and Nonna Laura decided to use Snow as their last name, to make it easier. Nonno Olindo's family name is Angelini. Many years later, after they had two beautiful daughters, if I do say so myself"—she grinned—"they also welcomed a granddaughter into the world, our dear Rayna, which means 'song of the lord.' Nonno Olindo liked to call her 'Rayna, the angel.'"

I was so glad that Aunty Jacq was telling me the All Souls' Day story that night. Hearing about family and our roots always made the world feel less like it was spinning out of control. It was kinda like life could make you forget who you were? And then you remembered again. All Souls' Day stories helped me remember that I did have roots somewhere, even if we were always getting pulled out of one place and put in another.

"One day Nonno Olindo went to work. He was laughing and telling a joke and pointing to a piece of wood and saying how silly it was to use inches instead of centimeters, and to not tell his wife he liked to make fun of the inglesi and americani for using inches. He was laughing really hard, and then he looked around at everyone and smiled, and then fell to the ground. Sudden heart attack."

"He died while he was laughing," I said.

"That's right. He died laughing," Aunty Jacq said. "After the funeral, Nonna Laura was feeling pretty lonely. She said that Nonno Olindo's ashes needed to be scattered into the sea. So she kissed her two daughters on the cheeks, and flew back to Italy to see the Adriatic."

"It's super salty, right?"

"That's right, Angel. It's super salty and very blue and beautiful."

I nodded.

"When Nonna Laura reached the sea, she divided Nonno's ashes. Half for the sea and half to be buried with her. She had a fisherman take her out on a boat, and she scattered some of Nonno Olindo's ashes into the Adriatic, and the next day, she placed the rest in their hometown's mausoleum.

"After saying her goodbyes to Nonno Olindo, she took herself out for a giant fish dinner. The Feast of the Seven Fishes in the middle of the summer, she called it. She told her daughters and baby Rayna all about her day, how she loved them, then went to bed. That night, she pulled the picture of Nonno Olindo out and laid it onto the pillow next to her and passed away peacefully in her sleep.

"That's when we all went to Italy, and you saw the Adriatic. We placed Nonna Laura's ashes in the mausoleum with Nonno Olindo, and then we came back to Boston. I had a good job in the museum then. I'm not sure if you remember it. And your mom really wanted to join the army and go into computers. Nonno Olindo and Nonna Laura lived their lives doing what made them happy, so that's what we did, too, and, well, you know the rest."

"Thanks, Aunty Jacq," I said.

"Sure, Angel. You still want to look at all the pictures on Sunday?"

"Absolutely. But first, more Halloween," I said, hitting play on the movie.

And as if on cue, Spike wiggled out of his little pouch and did a full round of feet smelling. As *The Addams Family* played, we snuggled up together. It was one of the best Halloweens ever.

16

I woke up Saturday morning feeling a lot better. I still had the same familiar worry for my mom that I always had when she was gone, but things seemed brighter. It was even bright outside. The November sun streaked across my desk while I worked on my latest pair of Converse and Spike snoozed in his cage. I smiled, hoping the shoes would dry quickly enough to wear on Monday.

That morning Aunty Jacq had made us simple buttermilk pancakes, soft-boiled eggs, toast, and tomatoes. It was like Aunty Jacq was making up for all the candy we'd eaten the night before. I pulled out my Sharpies and prepared to do the final outlining of the *Coco*-inspired Day of the Dead skulls on the heels. They would be perfect to wear in November.

Then the doorbell rang.

"Rayna! You have guests!" Aunty Jacq called from the door.

What? Impossible.

I set my markers down, looked over at Spike, and shrugged, then went to see what was going on.

Aunty Jacq held the front door open for none other than Marcie, Kevin, and Matt. The twins looked so much alike, I could barely tell them apart.

"Hi, Rayna," Marcie said. "We remembered that you were entering the VFA's pet talent show, and we thought maybe . . . Well, we thought that maybe we could all team up and help each other?"

My stomach turned. First, I actually had forgotten all about the contest, and second, no way would I like to "team up" with anyone.

Marcie must have read the answer on my face. She looked away from the door and down the street.

"Oh. Well, I am, but it's not till March, and, well, I haven't really thought about it."

"I'm sure—"

"—we can help," Matt and Kevin said.

"Guys, we can figure it out—" Marcie began.

"Would you all like to come in for an afternoon snack?" Aunty Jacq interrupted.

I glared at her, feeling wholeheartedly betrayed ... even though I knew she was just being nice.

Marcie's face lit up. "Thank you, Ms.—" Marcie said.

"Just call me Jacq," she said, gleaming. "Or Aunty Jacq. I just made some brutti ma buoni. They're Italian. You like cookies?"

Everyone nodded, except me. *Now what am I supposed to do?*

We all went into the kitchen, filing in around the island. Aunty Jacq placed a big platter of cookies in the center. They were for All Souls' Day on Sunday—something that was supposed to be just for us, but was sadly becoming treats for neighbors who should've been minding their own business.

Everyone grabbed a few cookies.

"What would you like to drink, lovelies?" Aunty Jacq asked.

A few minutes later, we all had our own preferred drink in our hands. But instead of talking, we were just standing there looking at each other like we'd all grown antlers out of our heads.

"I'll leave you to get down to business," she said, eyeing me with a look that said I should be polite—a good host for my guests.

Marcie took a bite of her cookie and then set it down on the island. She brushed off her hands and sighed. "We thought it would be good to help one another for the contest," Marcie began. "By teaming up, our pets will put on a better show and the event will be a lot more successful so the VFW will raise more money."

I was getting the feeling that this hadn't been her idea.

"You're entering your hedgehog, right?" Matt asked.

"How do you know that?" I asked in return.

"Well, Wilma said—"

"—you had a hedgehog," Kevin finished, taking two more cookies and handing one to Matt.

"So Matt and Kevin thought maybe you'd want to work together. We could help you come up with its talent or something," Marcie followed.

"He's not really social," I said, even though it felt like fibbing because Spike had been super nice to Wilma.

I was nervous. If everyone had been talking to Wilma, and

Wilma had been talking to Nick, wouldn't they know about what happened in the library? Why were they being nice to me?

"Look, we were just thinking, maybe we could share some ideas," Marcie said. Matt and Kevin nodded. "We could tell you what we're planning first, if you like?"

Silent stare.

"We still can't decide which movie we want Gayle to perform a line from," Kevin said.

"I'm still saying *Toy Story*, but my brother here has doubts," Matt chided.

"Too many vowels," Kevin said.

Marcie rolled her eyes.

"I think we should have her say, 'I'm a doctor, not a magician,'" Matt said.

"What's that from?" I asked.

"*Star Trek*," they all said in unison.

"Well, why can't she learn both?" I asked.

Marcie's eyes lit up. "Gayle is kind of an old bird, but I bet she could learn more than one line." Marcie smiled at me for the first time since she'd arrived. "Plus, that would definitely keep you two from arguing."

Matt and Kevin looked at each other, then back at the group. "Fine, it's a deal."

"Your turn," Kevin said, looking at Marcie.

Marcie picked her cookie back up and took a bite, trying to ignore them.

"Go ahead," Matt said.

Marcie let out a small sigh. "Matt said it isn't fair that my dog Daisy is already trained," Marcie said, "but I read the flyer. It doesn't say it has to be a 'new' trick or talent."

I bristled. I did not want to help someone else train their dog. Not when I couldn't have one of my own. "Marcie's right. You don't have to teach a pet new tricks, just bring the tricks you have."

"Word," Kevin said.

"Word," Matt repeated.

"So how can we help you with your pet's talent?" Kevin asked me.

"Hedgehogs are cool," Matt said.

"It's okay. Like I said, I haven't really thought about it just yet, and it takes time for a hedgehog to even remotely be social. He needs more time." I hoped this would satisfy them, but instead it opened a can of worms.

"Could we meet him?" Kevin asked.

"What's its name?" Matt asked.

"Where do you keep him?"

"What do you feed him?"

"Guys, please, you're freaking her out," Marcie said.

Was the look on my face that telling? It was true, I was freaking out. Marcie gave me a knowing smile. I gave her a polite smile back.

"Um, he eats veggies, hedgehog food, and worms. His name is Spike, and I keep him in my room."

"Can we meet him?" Matt asked.

"I don't know if now—" I said, trying to stop what was starting to feel more and more like a home invasion.

"I read up on hedgehogs before coming over. I mean, I didn't know if you'd really want our help or anything. But I learned a lot of cool stuff. They are nocturnal most of the time, right?" Marcie asked.

I nodded.

She really didn't think I'd help. My mind raced with the realization, but I stood frozen there in stone.

Marcie took the lead. "If Rayna lets us see him, he'll

probably be asleep, so you two will have to be chill."

Oh no. No one is coming into my room. That was like my secret hideaway, a private sanctuary. Someday, when I left Frederick, I wanted to think back on my room as the place I did my art— not where friends came and went. Memories of sleepovers and games—and friends who turned out not to be friends—rushed into my mind.

Matt and Kevin stared at me like I was about to announce the lottery numbers. I supposed the sooner they saw Spike, the sooner they'd stop being so curious and leave me alone. So I pulled myself together. *Be polite,* I told myself.

"I'll show you what he looks like, but then I need to do some homework." The three nodded.

"Cool," Matt said.

"Cool," Kevin said.

I led them into my room and over to the cage. Spike was balled up, sitting at the entrance to his hiding space, half in and half out.

"Oh wow. He's adorable," Marcie said, "and a little bigger than I thought he'd be."

Matt bent down to get a better look. "If he sleeps all day,

that may be your biggest challenge. The contest is during the daytime, after all. What if he sleeps through it?"

I hadn't thought of that. The whole talent show thing was sounding more impossible. Plus, I had never trained an animal in my life.

"Why don't we test our theory," Marcie said. "Rayna, why don't you pick Spike up and see if he responds to you at all."

I gently opened the cage and placed my hands down underneath him, scooping him up and lifting him out of the cage. At first he acted like he usually did, sniffing my hand.

"That's cool," Kevin said.

"Yeah, his nose is so twitchy," Matt agreed.

When Spike heard their voices he sniffed the air and then hissed. I put him back down into his cage, and he immediately fled into his cubby space. That was all we were going to get.

"I don't know," Matt said. "Maybe he's not the right pet for a talent show."

Marcie looked at me with a worried face.

"Yeah," Kevin agreed. "Maybe you should skip it."

Anger flared inside me. Who did these boys think they were? They weren't experts on hedgehogs.

"You have Spike all wrong," I heard myself saying. "He's actually incredibly smart and can do all kinds of things. He's very good with people. You'll see."

Liar, my head screamed at me. All Spike liked to do was eat, run around, and smell things. The twins were probably right.

Marcie looked at me like she could read my mind, but said, "That's the spirit."

"If you say so," Kevin said.

"I *do* say so." I moved to the door of my room and looked back expectantly at them. Marcie quickly took the hint and followed.

"Come on, guys. It's going to take a while to teach Gayle two new phrases."

"Word," Matt said as they followed Marcie out of the room.

"Word," Kevin said.

17

It was a solidly orange Monday. If Frederick Middle School was big on Halloween, they were ridiculous about Thanksgiving. The purple and black bats and cats had been replaced with fall leaves in red and orange, golden hay bales, pumpkins, and turkeys.

I, too, had undergone a change. On Sunday, I had said goodbye—for a while anyway—to my purple hair and dyed it deep crimson red. It was good to have a change, a fresh start.

As usual, I was a little early to Mr. Toliver's class. I opened my textbook and reviewed my homework from the weekend, then pulled out my spiral notebook and pens. Ready.

Nick slid into his seat in front of me. I didn't even look up. *Focus on classwork,* I reminded myself.

"Hey," Nick said.

I looked up to find that he had turned around in his seat to talk to me. He still had that same bummed-out feeling about him. I wanted to tell him I was sorry right then and there, but all I said was "Hey."

"Listen, I owe you an apology," he began.

What? He's apologizing?

"That day in the library, when I got all offended . . . I jumped to conclusions about you and that wasn't fair. I used to move around a lot, and being the new kid, being a guy with a braid, being Indian, it wasn't always easy. I got made fun of a lot."

"People should be able to wear their hair however they want, any-time they want," I said, pointing at my new red hair. "Crimson red."

Nick smiled, apologies still in his eyes.

"I owe you an apology, too. We move around a lot, too, and sometimes I'm not so good at talking to new people, and I can be . . . distant."

"I totally get that," he said.

The tension from the past two weeks of not speaking to

one another began to melt away and evaporate out the room.

"I, um . . . I have a confession to make," I said, taking a deep breath and trying to look him in the eye. "I was actually jealous that day."

"Jealous?" Nick asked, surprised.

"Yeah. I, um . . . well, it's a long story, but you were talking about being able to stay home now. You know, your dad retiring. And I was . . . jealous."

"I get that, too," he said.

I looked him in the eyes, and I knew. I knew he really did.

"Friends?" I asked, a grin spreading across my face.

"Friends," he said, holding out his hand for a handshake.

I shook his hand and smiled.

Relief washed over my entire body. I was so glad that Nick didn't believe I had something against Native people. And maybe it was okay if I had one friend. Sort of a friend—not too close, but an ally my own age. My head spun as I tried to make peace with the idea.

As Nick took off his coat and settled in, a thought occurred to me.

"Hey, you don't have to tell me what's going on or anything, but lately you've seemed a little . . . bummed? If you ever need to talk about it . . . Sorry. I'm sure that's too personal. Never mind. I mean, no, I'm still here if you want to talk, but I'm just saying I'm not nosy or anything. I mean . . ."

Nick chuckled. "It's cool. I appreciate it. I'm not always cheery this time of year. On one hand, we've got some really cool tribal holidays in the fall. But there's also all this Thanksgiving stuff, and I don't know . . ." he said, his voice trailing off. He glanced up at the clock. "Yikes," he said, and quickly headed to the back of the classroom to hang his jacket.

Nick flew back to his seat and smiled at me right when Mr. Toliver entered the classroom.

I smiled back.

His long braid swayed slightly as it hung down his back. The shirt he wore had a large seven-pointed star with images of what looked like seven different masks around it. It read: CHEROKEE NATIONAL HOLIDAY AND POWWOW.

I heard Mr. Toliver talking about what we had read over the weekend, but my head was elsewhere. If Nick and I did become friends, and if I could keep it together and not feel like Jell-O when he smiled at me, I realized I had a lot to learn about Nick and his culture, his family.

18

Can't they take a hint? I couldn't believe my space was being invaded on the bus ride home from school. It's not like I had been super friendly to Marcie, Kevin, and Matt over the weekend. One potential friend or ally or whatever I was going to call Nick was enough. Why did these three have to get all up in my business every chance they got? The front of the bus was supposed to be a safe space, and now here they were, surrounding me like a bunch of chicks with a hen.

"Are you turning in your entry papers for the talent show tomorrow?" Kevin asked me.

Matt and Marcie looked at me expectantly. I hadn't noticed it before, but Marcie had also changed her appearance. Her glasses were the same shape, but a different color. If we were friends, I'd tell her they looked cool, but we weren't, and I was annoyed she and the twins were even next to me.

"Yes," I said flatly, then looked away. I knew I was giving them the cold shoulder, but geez.

"Listen, Rayna, you had some real good ideas the other day, and we were wondering if you'd like to help us?" Matt asked.

No.

"We've been having a problem with Gayle," Kevin said.

"Since this last weekend?" I asked, incredulous.

"Yeah. She's been ignoring us for some reason, trying to avoid us."

I wonder why.

"It's okay, Rayna. Sorry to bother you. Come on, guys, let's go sit down."

So it definitely wasn't your idea to talk to me.

Matt ignored Marcie. "We thought Gayle might need to meet some new people. Maybe she's bored being in the house with us all the time," Matt explained.

"So if you could come to our house today and meet her—" Kevin began.

"—maybe she'll perk up, you know, open up? Make friends?" Matt finished.

You've got to be kidding me. Going to their house to meet their pet parrot was the very last thing I wanted to do. But Kevin and Matt really did look worried. Why was I even noticing that? *Don't do it Rayna, don't.*

"Okay," I heard myself say with zero emotion.

"Really?!" Marcie sounded very surprised by my answer.

"This is great. You'll come over later? Be our guinea pig?" Kevin asked.

"Um, today?" I asked.

"Yeah, the sooner the better," Matt said.

"It's the house with the big oak tree," Marcie reminded me.

"Right. Okay, I'll come by after I check in with Aunty Jacq," I said. I couldn't believe I was saying yes to this. But maybe this would keep them from randomly showing up at my door.

When the bus stopped, the trio headed out in front of me, but then Marcie hung back. "This is really nice of you. I know we're probably not the kind of people you would normally hang out with."

What did she mean by that?

"You know, the Star Trekkie, geeky, going to Space Camp

type? You seem like you're more an edgy, emo, cool-girl kind of person?" She looked over at me expectantly.

"Oh, I don't think—" I began.

"It's just this town is really small, you know? Not like living out in the country or anything, but small enough that it's exciting to have someone new around who seems to like pets?"

Was that a question? "I think animals are cool," I said.

"I knew it!" Marcie said, lighting up like the first time I met her. "Me too."

"I'm just not always a people person," I said, leaving out the fact that I was purposefully trying very hard not to be one. Before everything happened with my so-called friends in Pensacola, Aunty Jacq always said I could talk to anyone. But that was then. Now alarm bells were going off in my head.

The light in Marcie's face had dimmed a bit with my comment, but then lit back up again. "That's okay. That just means you're an introvert. We learned all about it at Leadership Camp."

"There's a Leadership Camp?"

"Yeah. Not as cool as Space Camp, but still fun," Marcie said as Matt and Kevin disappeared through their front door. "See you later?"

"Um, yeah." I turned toward my house and climbed up the wooden porch steps, feeling conflicted about my plan to avoid making friends, focus on my grades, and convince Mom to get me the dog of my dreams.

"Surprise!" she said as soon I opened the door.

"Mom! You're home!" I dropped my book bag and gave her a hug. It didn't matter how angry I could get with her or how I hated it when she left for weeks or months at a time. I was always happy to have her home.

"Yes, Angel, I am. It's so good to see you. What is that? Crimson red?" she asked, tugging on a strand of my hair.

"You better believe it," I replied. I called out a hello to Aunty Jacq, who had her head buried in the pantry, then dropped my bag by the door.

"I have some good news," Mom said, helping me take off my coat. "They've got me working these next couple of weeks here in Frederick at Fort Detrick, and then . . ." she said, pausing and rubbing her hands together like a villain with a secret plan, "I have all of Thanksgiving weekend off. No work! Woo-hoo!"

I laughed. "That's awesome, Mom. I'm glad."

"And," she said, "it's not confirmed yet, but my SO told

me this morning that it looks like my request for leave during Christmas will probably go through. So, fingers crossed."

"Fingers crossed," I said back.

"How's Spike?" she asked, looking toward my room.

"He is an odd animal." I smirked. "He loves those worms! And feet. He's really into feet."

"Well, that's good, I guess?" Mom asked, following me into my room and over to Spike's cage.

"He's coming around. He really loves his pouch. I've been putting him in it each night after dinner."

My mom's face was full of pride and approval. "That's wonderful! So glad Spike is finally starting to feel at home."

"He is." I nodded, sitting down on my bed and grabbing one of my black, fuzzy pillows.

"And how's school going?" she asked, sitting next to me.

"It looks like a Thanksgiving bomb went off in the hallways," I said.

"Sounds like Frederick Middle School has a decorating czar," Mom said, smiling. "And your schoolwork?" she asked.

"I'm all caught up, finally, if that's what you mean."

"That is, indeed. Rayna, I'm so glad you're adjusting okay."

I bristled. I didn't want to talk about "adjusting." People only had to adjust to something when it was new, and I Hated it with a capital *H*, so I changed the subject. "I have to turn in that entry form for the talent show. I've filled it out, but you need to sign it." I got up and retrieved the paper from my desk drawer and handed it to her.

"Okay, what do we have here," she said, reading through it. "Under talent you have 'responds to voice commands—and spreads cuteness everywhere.' That last part sounds about right! But is he responding to your voice?"

"Not yet, but if what Justin said at the store is right, he will."

"And how often have you been practicing with him?" she asked.

"Well . . ." I said, knowing that I'd been avoiding putting in the work with my hedgie, "I wanted to give Spike time to get used to me."

"I see," she said, probably seeing right through me. "All right, then, do you have a pen?"

"Me? In all my wonderful art supplies, you think I have a silly pen? That's so basic," I teased, getting up and grabbing a pen from the container on the desk. Mom got up, swiping it from my hand, and then signed the paper.

"I'll drop it off at the VFA, smarty," she said with a wink.

"Thanks. Oh, Mom, would it be okay if I went across the street to a neighbor's house for an hour?"

"Which neighbor?" she asked, sounding surprised.

"Matt and Kevin—they're the sixth graders that live across the street—they asked me on the bus today if I would come over to meet their parrot. It's ridiculous, I know, but they want to see how Gayle reacts to new people."

"Gayle?" My mom chuckled. "That's some name for a parrot. Sure, Angel, go on ahead. I've left Jacq with a ton of groceries to put away. Be home by dinner?"

"Yep," I said. I took another quick look at Spike. As usual, he was asleep. In another hour or so he'd be ready for company.

But was I ready for company? I looked out my window at the Stones' house across the street. Their big oak tree had nearly shed all its leaves. When I thought about going over there, my belly churned. But I couldn't ditch them.

So I took a big breath and headed across the street, tucking all my fears deep into my pockets.

19

It was just plain weird standing in Kevin's and Matt's room. The place was gigantic, with two twin beds pressed up against opposite walls and tons of space in between. There were two desks with chairs next to the two beds. If Kevin and Matt were mirrors of each other, so were their sides of their room. *Doctor Who* and *Star Trek* posters covered the walls, along with NASA images of planets and stars.

Gayle sat by the window in a large white cage. Even weirder than being inside a strange space with a large gray parrot was the fact that I was surrounded, literally from all sides of the room, by people—not just Matt, Kevin, and Marcie, but also

Wilma, who sat near the door scrolling through her phone. Other than seeing her that one time with Nick, we really hadn't talked much since the barbecue. She looked the same. Same nose ring, same hair pulled up high in a ponytail. Same eyeliner.

It was me who felt different than the last time I'd seen her. My armpits were sweaty and my mind raced. Had Nick told her we'd made up? Did she know that I wasn't a racist? Did I need to apologize to her, too? *Oh my god, what am I going to do?*

"So they convinced you to come, too, huh?" Wilma asked, looking up from her phone briefly to give me a knowing grin.

Thank god she doesn't hate me. "Yep," I said, grinning back. Then I turned to Matt and Kevin expectantly. "So, I'm here. What do you need me to do?"

"They've tried everything," Marcie said, taking over. "Gayle just seems bored. She's not responding to anyone. All she does is turn away and show you her tail feathers. She's never really acted like this before."

"Is she sick or something? Maybe you just need to take her to the vet?" I asked.

"We already tried that. The veterinarian said she was perfectly healthy—" Kevin began.

"—but that she may also be getting old," Matt finished.

I nodded. "So you think that because I'm new, she'll be curious and perk up?"

"Exactly," Matt said.

Gayle, I know exactly how you feel. Everyone up in your space, expecting you to do new things, meet new people.

I slowly walked over to where she sat on a long rung that ran across the full width of her cage. She turned an eye in my direction.

"Hey, Gayle," I said. I could feel everyone's stares burrowing into my back. "We haven't met before. I'm Rayna. I live across the street." *First I have to talk to hedgehogs, and now parrots.* I kept my voice easy so I wouldn't frighten her. "Matt and Kevin told me you needed someone new to talk to. So . . . hello."

Gayle bowed down and turned her head to the side to get a better look at me with that one eye. "Hello," Gayle said back.

"Yes!!" Matt and Kevin screamed together.

Marcie clapped, and Wilma fully looked up from her phone.

All the noise just made Gayle squawk and fly around in her cage, jostling its contents.

"Quiet down," I whispered, holding up my hands. "You're stressing her out. Sheesh." As soon as everyone was quiet again, I looked back over at Gayle, who was pacing from one end of her perch to the other.

"Sorry about that, Gayle," I told her. "Not everyone likes a commotion. Sometimes we just need some calm, some peace and quiet, right?"

My soothing voice seemed to settle Gayle down until she was only shifting her weight from one foot to another.

"Hey, girl," I said, trying to coax her into responding. "How are you feeling today?"

But she turned her back to me, and I knew, I just knew, Gayle wasn't saying another word. "I think she got too scared. She isn't going to talk to me again."

"But you got her to say something. That's more than we've done," Kevin said.

"If she doesn't talk to you, I don't know if we'll get her out of her funk," Matt said.

So *that* was why they kept bothering me? They just needed to give Gayle a diversion. I relaxed a little. Maybe they weren't really trying to be my friends.

I thought I'd feel great about that possibility, but for some reason it stung.

"At least she seemed interested in you for a minute. I've been worried, like maybe Gayle was . . . you know . . . heading to birdie heaven or something," Marcie said.

"Don't say that!" Matt said.

"Jeez, Marcie!" Kevin said.

"What? The doctor said she was an elderly parrot. I love Gayle. I'm just saying . . ."

"Not cool, Marcie," Kevin and Matt said in unison.

I could feel Marcie's desperation.

"How about I come by tomorrow and try again?" I suggested. *Wait. Why am I offering this?* I looked at Gayle. She seemed really gentle and nice and, well . . . sweet. I didn't want her distressed. And even though I didn't want to admit it, I didn't want Marcie distressed either.

"Would you?" Marcie asked. "You're not too, um, busy?"

Marcie was giving me an out. Why would she do that? I

didn't care. I was going to take it. My gut churned. "I mean. I think tomorrow's okay," I said, backpedaling.

"If you're able to come, that would be awesome. Right, guys?" she asked.

Kevin and Matt both nodded, then whispered together, "Awesome."

I was feeling more uncomfortable by the minute. Then Wilma stood up. "I gotta head out. Homework. Check you guys later," she said, giving us all a quick wave and slipping through the door.

I *had* to get out of there, too. This had been the longest fifteen minutes of my life. "I'm out, too. See you all tomorrow. Bye, Gayle."

As I made my way through the Stones' house toward the front door, Marcie called out to me. "Hey, Rayna!"

I stopped and turned around. "Yeah?"

"It was really nice of you to help today," she said, pushing her red glasses up her nose. "Gayle's been around for so long, and it's just been hard lately. The guys have been feeling sad and scared about what's happening to her, you know?"

I couldn't imagine having a pet your whole life and then

thinking you could lose it. "Sure," I said, "I understand."

Marcie smiled. "Thanks, Rayna," she said, her eyes gleaming once again.

Out on the front porch, Wilma was talking on the phone. "Gotta go, Dad . . . I know. It's in the fridge . . . okay, bye."

"That was wild," I said as we headed down the porch steps together.

"Yep," she said.

"What did Gayle do when you talked to her?" I asked, curious what had gone on before I arrived.

"Absolutely nothing. She just gave me that side-eye," Wilma said. "You're really good with animals, it seems."

"You think so? I don't know, I mean, I'd like to think I am. I've wanted a dog for so long, but my mom says I'm not ready for the responsibility."

We walked down the curving sidewalk to the end of Kevin and Matt's front yard.

"Well, you have a calm disposition. I think that's good for animals. How's Spike doing, by the way?"

"He's good." I grinned. "He poops a lot. I didn't realize hedgehogs were little poop machines. And he has a thing for feet."

Wilma cracked up.

I smiled. It actually felt good to make someone laugh.

"See you tomorrow on the bus?" Wilma asked as she headed down the sidewalk toward her house.

"Definitely," I called to her, and headed back across the street, back to home.

True to my word, I went over to Kevin's and Matt's the next day. Gayle had been cautious, but she'd also had more to say. After saying "Hello," she'd inched closer to me and asked, "Would you like some water?" Gayle was a very polite parrot. So, I'd sat down next to her and talked to the lady parrot. It felt a bit like visiting someone in a retirement home—awkward, but nice.

After a one-sided conversation where I'd rambled on about nothing, I thanked the twins for inviting me and hustled on home. I still wasn't comfortable hanging out with a group of peers. But like Gayle, I was polite.

20

For a lot of Americans, Thanksgiving meant cooking tons of food, but for my family, it also meant packing it all up to give to other people. Thanksgiving wasn't only about being thankful for what you had, but giving your time to pay it forward. I didn't mind. I actually liked how we spent Turkey Day. It got me out of my own head so I could concentrate on doing something nice for others. We'd spend time visiting with men and women at a VA hospital or medical center, a VFW in town, or an Elks Lodge. Our mission was to lift someone's spirits.

The vets we met stuck with me. Young soldiers coming back from a tour of duty always seemed a little lost, like their bodies were home, but in their minds they were still traveling and hadn't yet touched down on American soil. Older vets usually had great stories to tell, and new recruits were amped to get out and see the world!

Thinking about it, I couldn't remember the last time we'd just sat and ate a Thanksgiving meal at home together. Aunty Jacq said that since my grandparents hadn't celebrated Thanksgiving in Italy, it hadn't been a big holiday for them growing up.

When my mom, Aunty Jacq, and I arrived at the medical center, there was a big tent outside in the parking lot for veterans and their families to gather and share. The tables were packed— warming trays held heaping helpings of mashed potatoes and dressing, which bookended the carving station and coolers full of tea and water. And there were a ton of pies. Aunty Jacq had made four for the occasion. I hoped one would be left over so we could take it home just for us.

I helped put out the napkins and utensils with Aunty Jacq while my mom mingled. It was a little chilly in the tent, but the festive feeling inside made everything cheerful and cozy.

"Hey," a voice said.

I turned around to find Nick smiling at me. My knees

wobbled. His smile just did that to me. There was nothing I could do about it. I looked down at my Converse—a red pair with classic little skulls—and got ahold of myself.

"Hey," I replied, giving him a small smile. Just then a four-legged critter with a wagging tail leaned up against me. "And, well, hey to you," I said, reaching down to pet the pup.

"This is Mr. Unega, and he's extremely disappointed that he doesn't get to eat everything in this tent." I remembered Nick telling me about him and how angry I had become. Looking down at Mr. Unega now, there was no way I'd ever have hard feelings. He had a longing on his face that told me how much he wanted some turkey, and his little howls expressed his frustration that he wasn't getting any.

"I totally understand, Mr. Unega. But it's nice to meet you, anyway." I crouched down to his level and gave him all the pats he could take. "He's adorable," I said.

"Thanks," Nick said. "I was surprised to see you here. I don't see many people from school at our events."

"My mom is a die-hard support-the-veterans kind of soldier." I pointed at her as she talked to a couple she seemed to know.

"That's your mom?" Nick asked.

"Yeah, why?"

"She's talking to my parents."

"Oh, really?" They all seemed so happy to see each other. "I wonder how they know each other."

"I'm sure we'll get an earful," Nick said, grinning at me with an even bigger twinkle in his eye. "You know, before I saw you, I was sent out here to make some plates of food for the vets who can't make it outside to the tent. Want to help me dish up some food and make some deliveries?"

"Uh . . . yeah," I said. *Like absolutely of course I would love to,* I thought.

"I just need to give Mr. Unega to my pops."

I watched him walk across the tent to his folks and hand his dad the leash. I turned away so my mom wouldn't be able to get my attention and call me over. I was just getting to know Nick. I wasn't up for meeting his parents yet!

"Ready?" Nick asked, back at my side.

"Ready," I said, glancing down again at the little skulls on my shoes for strength. I felt happy but nervous, like a flock of birds were flying around inside my chest.

We found some empty foil pans, loaded up two plates into

each one, and carried them inside to the vets. Back and forth we went, four plates at a time, until everyone had lunch. We made a good team, actually, and I was feeling more relaxed the longer we were there. Then we went around taking dessert orders. Once everyone had pie, we gave each other a high five and left the medical center tired but happy.

"I totally need to chill for a bit," Nick said.

"Oh yeah, me too," I said, looking around to see where the chilling could be done. There were a few empty chairs in the corner of the food tent. "How about there?" I asked, pointing.

"Perfect."

We plopped down in the chairs, and I stretched my feet out in front of me as I kicked back. If I hadn't known better, I'd say the skulls on my shoes seemed happier than usual.

"You know, I really don't like Thanksgiving very much," Nick said.

"You mentioned something about that in class the other day. But you could have fooled me today. You seem to be having a great time," I said.

"That could be the company," he said, grinning.

The birds flying around my chest did somersaults.

"Don't get me wrong. I love helping out the vets and spending time with my parents. Taking care of our warriors and building good relationships is a very honorable and important thing. But being Cherokee, being Indian, makes the holiday . . . complicated."

I looked at him, trying to get my head around what he was saying.

"I can tell by the look on your face that you haven't heard someone talk about this before."

"Actually, no. But I'm all ears."

"Well, the whole first Thanksgiving story is a myth. I mean, there was a meal with the Wampanoag and a harvest celebration, but it wasn't exactly like the one you've heard about. I don't know why we can't just have a holiday where we're grateful and eat together. Instead, people focus on this 'story' that's been told forever, and don't even bother to learn the real history. The truth is, history has a lot of terrible things in it. A lot of massacres. A lot of Native people pushed out of their homelands. People don't want to know the whole story."

I nodded. It was true we didn't talk a lot about what happened to Indigenous people in school.

"Then in November, everyone says it's Native American Heritage Month. Kids make little headdresses at school and talk about Native Americans for a few weeks. But it's usually only about a small part of our history instead of who we are today. And then, when November is over, we're invisible again."

That was tough to take in. I really felt for Nick in that moment. I quizzed myself. Did I only think about Native Americans in November? Before I met Nick? Yeah, I think I did, which made me feel kind of guilty. I knew that there were Indigenous people here long before my grandparents arrived, before any Europeans arrived, but the only time I ever thought about it was in history class or at Thanksgiving. We were always just forgetting them. I felt unhappy and guilty and angry about what I was learning, but mostly I was sad for my friend. No wonder he had been bummed lately.

"That's really awful, Nick. I'm sorry that I don't know much about Native Americans. I don't even know how many I've met before."

"Thanks. It is what it is," he said, growing quiet.

"Yeah, I guess so. But I'm glad you're telling me, you know? To know some of what it's like to be Native American, to be Cherokee."

His eyes softened and warmed. "I don't want to upset you or anything. Today has turned out awesome. I'm glad you came, Rayna."

I could feel my face turning as crimson as my hair. Thankfully, before the birds flew around my chest again, we were distracted by the cutest and friendliest dog ever. Mr. Unega had run over and leapt up into Nick's lap, licking his face. I looked back to find Mr. Smallwood smiling in our direction. He gave me a little wave. I smiled back.

21

It was a few weeks later, and Thanksgiving had come and gone. Like clockwork, the decoration czar at FMS had transformed the autumnal hallways into a winter holiday extravaganza. The place was twinkling with every kind of holiday light: menorahs for Hanukkah, stringed Christmas lights, and kinaras for Kwanzaa. The place was Lit with a capital *L*.

There would be no homework, no tests till after the new year. Excitement filled the hallways, the classrooms, and spilled outside onto the school grounds. After lunch, I rounded the corner to the seventh-grade lockers to find Nick standing sheepishly in front of mine. I couldn't help but smile.

"Hey," he said as I drew near.

"Hey," I said back, feeling my cheeks flush.

"Did you ever notice that your locker is the number for pi?"

"That has been brought to my attention," I said, chuckling.

"Let me guess . . . Marcie?" he asked.

"The one and only," I said, opening up my locker and setting my math book inside.

"She is crazy smart. Did you know that she's been to Space Camp? It's sort of like NASA for kids? She wants to be an astronaut someday."

"Yeah, she told me about that. I definitely like making good grades, but I have no idea what I want to do when I'm older," I said, busying myself inside my locker, arranging things so I wouldn't have to look into Nick's eyes and feel all the feels.

"Really? You're a killer artist," he said.

"Maybe," I said, finally shutting my locker and giving him my full attention. "So . . . what brings you to locker three-one-four?" I asked.

"Well, I've been thinking about the conversation we had on Turkey Day, when I bummed you out with all my 'Indian-talk,'" he said, using air quotes.

"Wait, what? No way, you didn't bum me out. Well, maybe a little, 'cause some of what you told me about Thanksgiving sucks. But you also made me think about things, you know?" I realized I'd reached up to him while talking and was now touching his arm. I pulled my hand back. "Plus . . . um . . . I mean, thanks. I learned something new."

He nodded with a glint in his eye. I resisted rambling. "Um . . . I think we should get going? We're going to be late to our last class."

"Right, right. One sec, I have a holiday gift for you," he said, pulling his backpack around him and reaching inside. "If you *really* want a depressing read about Native people, I've got just the thing."

I chuckled and then felt bad for chuckling. "Sorry," I said. "I didn't mean to laugh at—"

"It's all good," he said, smiling. "Giving you a depressing book is totally ridiculous. But it's what no one teaches us at school." He handed me the book. It was called *An Indigenous Peoples' History of the United States for Young People*.

I looked back up at Nick. Our eyes met for a second. The warm turquoise color seemed to wash all over me. He trusted me. He was sharing something that meant a lot to him.

"Thank you," I said, still holding his gaze.

VRRRIIINNNNGGG!! The last-period bell sounded, pulling us out of the moment.

"Yikes!" I said, laughing.

"Oh man. Math quiz! I gotta run," he said, turning to head down the hallway.

"Good luck!" And with that, we were just part of the rush of all things middle school.

Exactly one hour later, we were free. Free to pretend school didn't even exist in our universe! Free to hang out and do whatever we wanted. The hallways were in chaos, and the teachers didn't seem to mind at all. I guess they were free, too!

I walked out of the school building and headed toward the bus. It had turned chilly outside, so even though the sun was still shining, I pulled my hoodie up over my head. The air felt fresh and clean. I loved winter breaks. And for this break, I had a plan. Over the past few days, I'd admitted to myself that it was time—time to train my hedgehog.

Justin at the pet store had been pretty clear about how hedgehogs take a while to trust their owners, but I knew Spike had warmed up to me. Now I was counting on something else Justin had said: Hedgehogs eventually learn to come when called. I hoped that was true.

I climbed onto the bus and took my usual seat. Looking out the window and watching everyone hanging out and laughing in the school parking lot, I felt the joy of the day dim inside me. I tried not to feel envious of how easy everyone seemed to have it. How relaxed they were. I knew I wasn't the only military kid in the school, but off base, I could feel how much closer people seemed to be to one another—how they all seemed to take for granted the time they had together.

"Hey, Rayna," Marcie said, passing me and taking a seat a few rows back.

"Hey," I called back.

Matt and Kevin followed her.

Since I'd been spending time with Gayle, the three of them had begun sitting closer to me on the bus, and I'd become used to listening to them. I'd discovered that they all *really* loved *Star Trek*. More than I ever imagined. So much so, they'd gotten into an argument that left them not talking to each other for a week. It'd been super weird, because I realized that listening to them had become normal for me—part of Frederick feeling more like home.

What set them off into silence had been a huge debate about whether Captain Janeway in *Star Trek: Voyager* was as good a captain as Captain Picard in *Star Trek: The Next Generation*. Marcie had insisted that the only reason Matt and Kevin thought Captain Picard was better was because he was a guy. Even though I wasn't a Trekkie, I'd seen both shows and she was right. Their reasons were weak. There had been a few moments when I'd wanted to step in and tell Kevin and Matt just that, but I'd kept silent. Sci-fi shows—all that space-time continuum stuff—was what bonded them together, even while fighting. I wasn't a part of that bond, and I'd told myself that I would never be. So I'd stayed out of it.

But I was glad they were talking again.

"Hey."

I looked up. It was Wilma.

"Hey," I said.

"Do you mind if I sit up here with you today?" she asked, looking at me with a tired expression. Her sparkly eyeliner was cheerier than she was.

"Sure," I said, moving my book bag out of the way so she could sit down.

"Is it just me, or has the school kind of overdone it with the holiday decor?"

I chuckled. "It's not just you."

The bus driver climbed in and looked back at us all. He checked his watch, then sat down in his seat and shut the bus door.

Something about Wilma seemed different. I tried to figure it out without staring at her, but it was difficult. Finally, it hit me. She didn't have her phone. I wanted to ask her about it, but thought it might be too personal. Wilma never said much about herself.

I tried to think of something to talk about while the driver turned on the engine and maneuvered the bus through the school parking lot.

"How's Spike?" Wilma asked.

"He's good, but . . . I have to start training him to do something for the VFW talent show. The guy at the pet store said it takes a while to train a hedgehog, so I can't wait till the last minute."

"Smart," Wilma said. "What are you going to train him to do?"

"I said he responds to voice commands on the entry form, but . . ."

Wilma smirked. "He doesn't?"

"Not yet. It wasn't really a *lie* lie. More like a hopeful future truth?"

Now Wilma chuckled.

I began to relax, forgetting my walls. "I have it all planned out. Over winter break, I'm going to set up a table in the backyard and see if I can teach him a trick. I have his favorite treat ready to go."

"Worms?"

"Yeah. You remembered."

"Hard to forget. Worms and feet," Wilma said, grinning.

"I have no clue what I'm doing," I confessed.

"Sounds like you could use a hand."

I really did prefer keeping to myself most of the time—but getting a little help with Spike, well, that would be . . . helpful.

"Yeah," I said, conceding.

"I'm so glad you asked!" Wilma said, sitting up taller in the seat. "I'd be happy to help you train Spike."

I was in shock. Wilma wanted to hang out? She'd never asked me to hang out before. Panic rose in my chest. She was the kind of person who took friendship seriously. And I was avoiding friends, except with Nick, maybe . . .

Something stirred in me. It had been a long time since I'd hung out with a girl my own age who was into the same things as me. Well, at least I thought Wilma might be in to the same things. Our clothes were kind of edgy, she seemed to like art, and we had a similar sense of humor. And she wasn't like Marcie, Matt, and Kevin—who you could tell had been best friends since birth. Wilma was always on her own. Like me.

"Of course, if you really don't need it . . ." she said, pulling on the frayed edges of her ripped-up jeans.

I could feel my heart and my head arguing with each other.

Head: *Stay alone, it's safe.*

Heart: *Make a friend, it's what you want.*

Stay alone . . .

Make a friend . . .

My pulse raced. I didn't want to lose this chance to get to know Wilma better. Even if that meant I had to break my rules. I'd broken them with Nick already. Why couldn't I do it again? My heart won. "Are you kidding?" I said, elbowing her. "I need a miracle. Wilma the miracle."

"Cool." Wilma smiled, her eyes finally matching her sparkly makeup.

22

The next morning, I woke up feeling lighter and happier than I had in a while. Maybe it was because it was the holiday break, or because Nick didn't hate me? Or maybe it was because Wilma wanted to hang out. I didn't know, but it felt good to feel good.

I ignored the scaries forming in my belly. I was tired of that feeling. It wasn't gone completely, but at least it was quieter.

After the bus ride the day before, Wilma and I had sat on my porch and planned Spike's training. I nearly got up the courage to ask her about her phone—if everything was okay—but it didn't seem like the right time, not when she was so excited to help train Spike.

We'd decided to hold our trainings in the afternoons around

five. Since it was getting darker earlier, and Spike was more nocturnal, we knew he'd be more alert then. Wilma had the brilliant idea of moving his practice time up a little bit each training session, so eventually we might get him to be alert as early as three in the afternoon. The talent show was between three and five, so if we could get him comfortable during that time, maybe, just maybe, he'd be fully awake for it.

But first, there were Saturday pancakes. An Aunty Jacq tradition. I threw back the covers on my bed, pulled on some cozy socks and a hoodie, and headed to the kitchen.

"Morning, Angel," Aunty Jacq said, standing over the skillet with a spatula in her hand.

"Morning," I said, sliding into the chair at the breakfast bar. "What flavor are we having today?"

"Apple and cinnamon," she said. "Something warming. It's freezing outside."

I took note of that. Maybe Wilma and I would have to work in the garage.

Aunty Jacq set a plate of pancakes in front of me and one for herself next to me. Then she climbed into her chair and we dug in. No matter what was happening, I always knew there would be pancakes on Saturdays, and I loved Aunty Jacq for that.

Mom was in San Diego. Thankfully, it was a trip where she could still call in the evenings and check in. So far, she had been told she'd be back by Christmas Eve and would get a few days' leave. But who knew? I doubted even the army was sure.

"I have some good news." Aunty Jacq smiled with a mischievous glint in her eye.

Was this really going to be good news, or something annoying she would try to convince me was good? Adults were always doing that.

"Your favorite aunty has been selected as one of five artists to have a showing at that art gallery downtown. You know the one by the pretty canal with all the water lilies?"

"Oh, Aunty Jacq!" I squealed. "That's amazing!" I got up and gave her a giant hug. "When is it? And how many pieces?"

"It's on Valentine's Day, so I only have two months to get ten pieces ready! I hope you'll help me pick out which ones to show?"

"Absolutely, I'm your gal," I said, settling back into my chair.

Aunty Jacq's phone rang in the living room. I continued to relish my pancakes as she got up to answer. It was my mom.

"Kate, what exactly does that mean?" I heard her ask.

Oh no.

"So then what day would that be? . . . Well, when will you know? . . . Okay . . . What do you think? . . . I know, I know, it's just . . ."

I heard Aunty Jacq sigh. *This isn't good,* I thought. I tuned out the rest of the conversation, swirling one of my last bites of apple pancakes around in maple syrup on my plate. *I knew she wouldn't be here for Christmas. I just knew it.*

Aunty Jacq hung up the call. I leaned back in my chair and peered down the hall. Aunty Jacq was standing in the middle of the room with her hand on her hip, staring wistfully at our newly lit Christmas tree.

My eyes began to tear, seeing her like that. I got up from the breakfast bar and went to her. "Aunty Jacq? You okay?" I asked, trying hard to be strong and not cry.

She turned toward me and held out her arms. I walked over to her and hugged her tight.

"What happened?" I asked.

"Oh, Angel. I'm sorry to worry you too much. Your mom's safe," she said, guiding me to the couch.

I knew what was coming. "I'm glad, but . . . Christmas isn't happening, is it?" I wasn't surprised to feel tears sliding down my cheeks.

"We don't know yet," she said. "Her commanding officer called her into a meeting today. Some kind of hack that 'affects national security' means she has to stay in San Diego for a while longer. They told her that her request for holiday leave was noted, but that was all they said."

"What if . . ." All my worries were rising in my chest. "She's always in San Diego lately. What if they make us move there? What if you can't do your art show? What about this house and . . . and . . ." I stuttered, unable to finish my questions.

Aunty Jacq's face filled with warmth and compassion. "Oh, my angel. You know what? Whatever they tell your mom, we're going to have a good Christmas. And one way or another, you and me will be here together on Valentine's Day for the show. Okay? How does that sound?"

I was quiet for a second. On the one hand, it felt good to know that Aunty Jacq would make sure we'd be in Frederick longer, *and* that Christmas wouldn't be an epic fail. But on the other hand, I hated the army. Hated it with a capital *H. And* I was angry at my mom. I didn't want to be, but I was. The idea of moving sounded terrible no matter what, no matter when.

I looked up and saw the worry in my aunty's eyes. Her curly, dark hair was escaping from her ponytail and drifting around her face. I didn't want her to worry or feel bad. It wasn't her fault that everything was falling apart once again. "Okay," I said at last.

"It will be fine, Angel," Aunty Jacq said, putting her arm around my shoulders. "You'll see. Christmas is going to be the bomb!"

That made me chuckle. "The bomb, huh? You know we really don't say that anymore."

"You kids. I can't keep up with your slang." She grinned.

That afternoon, Aunty Jacq and I painted while one of her favorite jazz albums played on the turntable in the living room. Our house had become an artist studio, with Aunty Jacq in her room at her easel and me in mine at my drafting desk.

Spike was buried somewhere in the sawdust of his cage, sleeping away as I worked on my latest creation—green high-tops with a white skull-and-crossbones and red eyes. Instead of two bones making the crossbones, these sported two candy canes. They were perfect for Christmas.

It felt good to paint. It was something no one could take from me. No matter where we lived, I'd always have my desk and my paints and my ideas.

After putting the finishing touches on the last candy cane, I set the shoes to the side to dry and cleaned up. It was already three o'clock, and I still needed to set up for Spike's training session.

Aunty Jacq had given me a six-foot folding table and some short wooden planks Mom had been using as edging in her someday-garden. I placed the tall, flat pieces of wood around the table's edge, so that it all looked like a shallow box without a top. Once everything was in place, I used duct tape to keep it all together. I dubbed the table "The Hedgie Gym."

Then I went back inside to see if the little guy was awake yet. Nope. "Five p.m., buddy," I said, "and then it's gym time."

At four o'clock, the doorbell rang. *Wilma must want to start early,* I thought. That was fine. Even though I was a tad nervous to really and truly hang out with Wilma, I was excited, too. I quickly shuffled to the door.

Nope. It definitely wasn't Wilma. The *Star Trek*/Parrot/
Science crew was standing on my front porch.

"See, I told you she'd be home," Marcie said.

"What's going on?" I asked.

"Tell her, Kevin," Matt said.

"You tell her," Kevin said.

Marcie sighed and spoke for the group. "Gayle is doing great.
She's starting to say 'To infinity and beyond' but she's also been
saying something else."

"Okay. Like what?" I asked.

"Well, I guess she really liked your voice when you came
over? Because she's been saying 'It's okay, Gayle' in your voice."

"My voice?" I asked, confused.

"Yeah, she has this thing for imitating voices. She can do
Mr. and Mrs. Stone's voices, and Kevin and Matt, and Worf
from *Star Trek*."

"What about your voice?" I asked, curious why Marcie
wasn't in the list.

"She totally talks 'Marcie,'" Matt said.

"Oh yeah," Kevin said. "She says 'Guys, guys, come on' just
like Marcie says all the time."

I couldn't help but chuckle at that. "I've only been there twice. Why would she imitate me?"

"We don't know. But a lot of times she'll start to say 'To infinity and beyond,' and then interrupt herself and say, 'It's okay, Gayle.' We thought maybe you could come over and repeat the *Toy Story* line to her? Maybe if she hears it in your voice, she'll want to mimic you and say it?" Marcie asked.

I hesitated. "I'm kind of busy today, but—"

"That's okay!" Kevin said. "How's tomorrow?"

"Or the next day?" Matt said.

"It *is* winter break," Marcie said, pushing her glasses up on her nose.

They looked so hopeful that I couldn't take it, and caved.

"Okay, I'll come by tomorrow."

23

An hour later, Wilma and I placed Spike right in the middle of the Hedgie Gym. Wilma wasn't dressed quite warmly enough, but she had on the coolest vintage T-shirt over a button-down flannel shirt, nineties style. The T-shirt was red with a giant worm on the front of it and read DUNE. She'd worn it especially for Spike, since he loved worms.

"Maybe we can start by seeing how fast he will come to me to get a worm," I suggested.

"That's a good idea," Wilma said, joining me on my side of the table and handing me a fresh can of the wriggling treats.

I reached into my jacket pocket, took out a pair of long

tweezers I'd found stored in Mom's first aid kit, and carefully used them to pick up a single worm.

"Hey, Spike," I said, holding it out to him. "Snack time."

Spike didn't move.

"Come on. I know you'll love munching this fatty here."

"Maybe we're too far away for him," Wilma said. "I read online that hedgehogs are a little blind. Maybe he can't see us or the worm."

"Good point." I moved closer to Spike and held the worm in front of his face.

Spike's nose began to twitch. He could smell it. Yumminess was nearby. He began to move toward me and the worm. "Good boy, Spike! Get that wormy."

He finally located his prize and quickly grabbed the little worm and chomped with glee.

"That's so gross, but so cool," Wilma said. She held out the can of worms for me to reach in and grab another. I moved farther away and called the hedgie again. "Spike, come this way. Snack time."

He pattered over to where I was, sniffed the worm, and then chomped on it with glee.

Spike wasn't going to be racing anywhere anytime soon. I could only get him to move if I held the worm about three feet away. Was that really a talent? Or did it only show that hedgehogs liked to eat?

Before I could coax him with another worm, Spike's nose went into overdrive. He wandered around the Hedgie Gym, lifting his nose to the air and sniffing. He even bumped into the side walls a few times.

"He really has the worst eyesight," I said, after another bump.

"And he's probably not used to all the different smells happening out here," Wilma concurred.

We watched him sniff and wander around a while longer.

"I say we call it a day," I suggested. "We can pick up again tomorrow if you want."

"Sounds like a plan," Wilma said, placing the lid back on the can of worms.

"Oh, wait, I also have to go over to Matt and Kevin's house tomorrow."

"You do?" Wilma asked. "I didn't think you liked them very much."

My heart fell. It wasn't that I didn't like people. I just didn't want to get involved with them. That's all.

"It's not that," I said. "I just . . ."

Wilma listened patiently.

"Moving around a lot sucks."

"I can imagine," Wilma said.

"Right before I came to Frederick, I had two close friends in Pensacola—Ellie and Jodie. I hung out with them all the time, like *all* the time. I thought they were really cool—nice and not fake or anything. And I felt lucky that I'd met them, because even though I was new and they'd grown up together, they accepted me. We spent so much time together . . . I thought they liked hanging out with me. That we were close friends, you know? But then last summer when I told them the army was making us move to Maryland, they were . . ." My throat started to close up. "They were . . ." I took a deep breath. "Unemotional. It was like I became invisible all of a sudden—that me moving didn't matter. *I* didn't matter. I told them I'd keep in touch and tried to plan lots of cool things to do together so we'd have a summer to remember, but they always had a reason why they couldn't meet up. And right before I moved, they totally ghosted me."

"That's harsh," Wilma said.

I straightened up and shoved my hands into my pockets. "I mean, it wasn't like I had been in Florida for very long. Ellie and Jodie were friends with each other way before I moved to town, like Kevin, Matt, and Marcie are, so I guess me leaving really didn't change much for them. When they stopped hanging out with me, things just went back the way they were for them."

Wilma was quiet, taking it in. "Losing people unexpectedly is hard."

I nodded.

"It's getting pretty windy out here, isn't it?" Wilma asked.

"Yeah, let's go in. Aunty Jacq promised treats for the trainers."

"Nice," Wilma said.

"Come on, Spike, let's go."

He lifted his little hedgehog legs and walked across the table to me.

Wilma's eyes were wide. "Did Spike walk over to you when you told him 'let's go?'"

"I think so."

"Try it again," Wilma said.

I moved to another corner of the table. "Spike, let's go," I said.

Spike turned his head in my direction, wiggling his nose, but didn't move. I repeated the command, and Spike continued to sniff in my direction.

"You can do it, buddy," I said. But the only thing moving was Spike's nose.

"Maybe he wants to, but feels a little lost. It *is* his first time outside," Wilma encouraged.

"True," I said, deflated.

"Don't worry. He's going to master the Hedgie Gym. Besides, he loves you."

I picked him up and put him in his pouch, which hung across my chest. He wiggled into it and then poked his head out. He was a cute little guy.

"Um, Rayna," Wilma said, rubbing her hands together to warm them.

"Yeah?" I asked, petting Spike under his chin.

"Treats? For trainers?"

"Right!" I chuckled. "Let's go in." And with that, Team Hedgie hustled back inside to the warmth of Aunty Jacq's kitchen.

24

I was glad Wilma came with me the next day to visit Gayle. We'd finished our Hedgie Gym time for the day, and Wilma suggested that maybe it would be good to put Spike in his carrying pouch and bring him with me. That way he could get used to the smells and sounds of other people. After all, on the day of the show, there would be an audience.

Standing in Kevin and Matt's room, Spike wholeheartedly disagreed. He burrowed himself deep into his carrying pouch and would only peek out for Wilma.

"He really is shy," Marcie said, watching Spike wiggle around. "But cute."

"Thanks," I said, feeling a little less guarded than usual. "So should I just sit next to Gayle like last time and talk to her?"

"Sure," said Kevin. He and Matt stood waiting expectantly by her cage. They were both sporting new fades. "We just need you to say 'To infinity and beyond.'"

"Okay," I said, bringing one of the desk chairs over. I tried not to think about all the eyes on me, but couldn't help glancing over at Marcie, who gave me a reassuring smile. When I looked back at Gayle, she was sitting on one of the rungs and slowly lifting one foot and then the other.

"Hi, Gayle," I said.

Gayle stopped lifting her legs and turned an eye toward me.

"How've you been?" I asked her.

The parrot's gray body and red tail feathers seemed to stretch and point in my direction.

"It's okay, Gayle. I'm a friend." *Right,* I thought. Hearing the word *friend* come out of my mouth sounded strange.

"It's okay, Gayle," the bird said back—in *exactly* my voice. My eyes shot wide. *Now that's bizarre!* I thought. *Stay calm for Gayle,* I told myself.

"Good," I said. "I'm glad you're okay."

"It's okay, Gayle."

"Kevin and Matt would like for you to say something new," I suggested.

"Click clack pop pop. New."

"Right, something new, Gayle."

"New Gayle," she squawked.

"Exactly. They want you to say 'To infinity and beyond.'"

Gayle cocked her head. "It's okay, Gayle," she said.

"Right. It's okay to say 'To infinity and beyond.'"

"Pop pop Gayle clack clack."

This wasn't going quite as smoothly as the twins had hoped. "To infinity and beyond," I repeated, enunciating each word.

"Clack clack. Want some water?"

I smiled. *Always so polite.* "I'm okay, Gayle."

"Okay, Gayle," she said.

"What if we said it with more gusto?"

"Gusto, Gayle."

"That's right, Gayle." I chuckled and gathered up some motivation. Then, trying my best to sound like Buzz Lightyear, I bellowed, "To infinity and beyond!"

"Clack clack! Beyond!"

"That's right, Gayle! To infinity and beyond!"

And then, exactly in my voice, Gayle cried, "To infinity and beyond!"

Everyone jumped up and shook their hands in the air, silently cheering while trying not to disturb Gayle's breakthrough.

"That's amazing," I told the bird in my most soothing voice.

"Amazing Gayle."

I beamed. She sure was. And maybe, so was I.

25

Mom made it home for Christmas. Literally—she arrived on Christmas Eve morning. At first, I was super glad to see her. When she burst through the front door, I ran to hug her, and everything felt warm and cozy and cheerful. But when I looked into her eyes, things changed.

I didn't know what it was, but Mom didn't seem like herself. She was distracted and quiet. Something wasn't right and it frightened me.

I kept reminding myself about what Aunty Jacq had said, that no matter what, we'd be in Frederick for her art show, which was still two months away. But the sadness in my mom's eyes told me there were all kinds of things—army things—that meant we wouldn't be able to say no if she told us we were moving again.

I didn't think Aunt Jacq noticed Mom's mood. She had been preparing and planning Christmas Eve dinner for days, which in our house was called *cenone della vigilia*. To properly carry on Nonno Olindo's tradition, there had to be seven different kinds of seafood prepared seven different ways, the Feast of the Seven Fishes.

Nonna Laura's family had a tradition, too: a proper Christmas pudding. Passed down from her English father, Aunty Jacq said a Christmas pudding could bring Nonna Laura to happy tears. When Mom and Aunty Jacq were little, everyone would open gifts after dinner, play cards until midnight, and then go to Mass.

Now we had our own tradition. "A little bit of the past, a little bit of the present," Aunty Jacq always said. We'd eat our fish dinner on Christmas Eve, open just one gift, and then settle in super snug to watch *The Nightmare Before Christmas*. The movie was, of course, my own addition to tradition.

After I helped Mom settle in, I was put straight to work in the kitchen. I had to peel shrimp, chop vegetables, and cut lots of lemons. We made fresh pasta. I helped Aunty Jacq lower a tied pudding into a steaming pot of water. One task after the other had to be done just right. It was real work, and the kitchen became hot; Mom had to open the windows.

At six o'clock, as we were finally nearing the end of all our preparations, there was a knock at the door. *Did Mom invite guests?*

I was a sweaty mess. My crimson hair stuck to my face and my shirt had flour and food all over it. I cracked open the front door to find Wilma on our porch. Happy to see her, I opened the door wide.

"Hey, Wilma," I said, smiling.

"Hey," she said. But she wasn't smiling back. Actually, when I looked more closely, her eyes were puffy and her eyeliner smeared.

"You okay?" I asked.

"No," she said flatly. Honestly.

I opened the door for her to come in. "Let's go to my room to talk, okay?"

She nodded.

Once inside, she went over to Spike's cage. "Hey, little guy," she said, her voice cracking. Spike was awake and munching away on some carrot slices I had put in his cage.

I sat down on the bed and waited for Wilma to open up. Whatever was going on with her must've been bad if she had come down to my house on Christmas Eve.

The room was silent for a minute. Then, just when I was about to ask her what was going on, she spoke. "I just didn't want to be home alone, again."

"Alone?"

"Yeah, my dad said he had to work, and that he'd be late, but I have that tracking thing on my phone, and he's not at his office. He's with Kentucky."

"On Christmas Eve?" I asked in shock.

"Yeah," Wilma said.

"I'm sorry, Wilma."

She slumped down in my desk chair and let it all out. "My mom passed away a year and a half ago. The doctors said she had a stroke, where a blood clot gets into your brain. It was very sudden. After that, my dad was depressed for a long time. I mean, we both were. But he would come home from work, go straight to his room, and stay there all night. I had to start making myself dinner and stuff. You know?"

I nodded. I couldn't imagine what that was like.

"I got used to being alone. Alone at home. Alone at school."

I definitely understood that.

"Then we moved to this block. We used to live in DC, but Dad said Frederick would be better for us, a place to start over. Only it was a lie. He only wanted to move so he could be near Kentucky. Her real name is Anne, but sorry, not going to call her that.

"Right before school let out, my dad found out that I was tracking him with my smartphone. He got mad and took it from me. He basically grounded me from using it. But today, after he said he wasn't coming home till late, I searched for it all over the house, and found it in one of his drawers. And guess where he was?"

"With Kentucky."

Wilma nodded.

"That really sucks, Wilma. I'm so sorry."

"I think I remind him of my mother, and he just can't be around me."

I couldn't help it. I teared up for Wilma.

My mom came in the room, full of Christmas cheer. "Rayna! I see you have some Christmas company!"

"I do," I said.

"It's good to see you, Wilma. Rayna said Spike's learning a lot with you around."

Wilma cleared her throat. "Yeah." I could tell she was trying to act like everything was okay.

There was no way I was going to send Wilma home alone on Christmas Eve. "Mom, would it be all right if Wilma has dinner with us?"

Mom seemed to catch on that Wilma wasn't doing so well. "Of course! The more the merrier. I hope you like fish, though, because that's about all we've got."

"All kinds," Wilma said reassuringly.

"But call your dad first, okay?" Mom requested. "If he's all right with it, then we're happy to have you."

"I will. Thanks."

Good thing Mom had a landline. Wilma called her dad, and not only did he say yes to letting her stay for dinner, he also said she could watch the movie with us, too.

Our cenone della vigilia was amazing. We ate so much I thought I was going to pop. And Wilma was such a sport. She even tried the fishy brodetto stew, which is, well, an acquired taste.

Right before we settled into the living room for the movie, I went and collected Spike. Of course, the WHOLE family had to be there. It was Christmas. He wandered about on the couch as I pulled up the movie on our TV.

Aunty Jacq was just drifting off in one of the living room chairs when suddenly she jolted herself upright. "I can't do it!" she said, laughing. "I'm sorry to break new traditions, but I'm beat! I need to sleep off this meal," she said, slowly getting up and stretching.

"Me too," Mom said. "I got on the plane before midnight last night to make it here on time today. Why don't you two—" She paused, looking down at Spike. "I mean, three—go on and watch the movie. Besides, how many times have I seen it now?" Mom asked, winking at me.

"Not enough," I teased. Maybe Mom had just been tired that morning. Maybe I'd been worried for nothing.

"Right," she said, giving me a little side-eye. "I think I'm going to head to my room and do a little reading before bed. I might even read something Christmassy. You two, have fun."

Wilma and I grabbed spots on each end of the couch and let Jack the Pumpkin King lead us in song. With Wilma and Spike around, I forgot all about not wanting friends. I was just happy that she was having a good time, and that Mom was home safe.

All of a sudden, my phone buzzed.

"Who's that?" Wilma asked.

"Probably my mom wanting me to bring her something."

I sat up and opened my phone.

It was Nick!

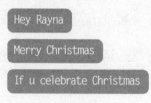

My face must have turned as red as my hair.

"So . . . it's not your mom," Wilma said.

"It's Nick," I said in a totally unnecessary whisper.

Wilma laughed. "Well, what does he want?"

"To wish me merry Christmas?"

Wilma smirked as my cheeks heated. "You gonna answer him?" she teased.

"Uh, I guess I should, huh?"

Hey Nick

Merry Christmas 2 U 2

If u celebrate Christmas

R u free tomorrow?

Yeah, I think so

Why?

On Christmas day my family always goes 2 a movie

My cousin was gonna go

But he doesn't want 2 C the new Marvel movie

I have an extra ticket

R u interested?

Don't want 2 interrupt family things

. . .

. . .

Let me ask my mom

Cool

My stomach rolled in somersaults like it was trying to leave my body and run for the hills. *Why would he text me? Did he* like *me, like me?*

"Spill," Wilma commanded.

"Nick asked if I want to see the new Marvel movie with his family tomorrow."

"Woo-hoo! He's, like, the best-looking and nicest guy in our grade."

"I don't know. I don't . . . I mean, it would be fun, but—"

"You said you'd ask your mom, didn't you?"

"Yeah," I said, sweaty and freaked out.

"Then go ask her."

Five minutes later, I left my mom's room with an ear-to-ear smile plastered on her face, and texted Nick.

Hey

Hey

My mom says I can go

. . .

. . .

. . .

That's great!

Ok I'll tell my dad

Pick u up at 2?

K

K

I headed back to the living room and leapt onto the couch, grabbing the remote.

"So . . ." Wilma inquired with anticipation.

"She said yes," I said, covering my face with my hands.

"Don't be shy! That's great."

I took a deep breath and looked through my fingers at her. "You think so?"

"What did I just say?"

I dropped my hands and smiled. "It's so crazy. Our parents actually know each other. His dad and my mom were in basic training together."

"It's fate, Rayna the Shy Girl," she said, smiling.

I threw a pillow at her. Spike did NOT like the projectile cushion attack, and hightailed it back into his pouch. Wilma and I just looked at each other and cracked up.

Late that night, long after *The Nightmare Before Christmas* and *Elf* had ended, there was a gentle knock at the front door.

"That's probably my dad," Wilma said, getting up from the couch and grabbing her black lace-up boots.

"I'll walk you out," I said.

She nodded and followed me to the front hall.

When we opened the door, her dad stood on the porch with a strange expression on his face. Was it guilt or sadness? I couldn't tell. "You must be Rayna," he said.

"Yes," I said. "And you're Mr. Ryan. Sorry you had to work late on Christmas." I looked over at Wilma, who was sporting a smirk. We knew what was up.

I felt someone behind me. It was my mom, pulling her robe around her and stepping slightly in front of me. "Mr. Ryan, thank you for letting Wilma join us tonight."

"Ms. Snow, hello, nice to meet you. Sorry I missed that barbecue you had this fall," he said, holding out his hand to shake hers.

"No problem. It's Sergeant Snow, but please, call me Kate."

"Kate, yes, of course. Thank you for having her. It's been a tough year at work," he lied.

Mom nodded.

"Let's get home, Wilma, so everyone can get some sleep. Bye now," he said, and headed down the steps with Wilma in tow.

"Bye," Wilma said, waving at us.

I waved back, letting my mom pull me back in through the door. As I shut the door, I watched Wilma and her dad walk down the quiet sidewalk. Together, but completely alone.

26

I had no idea what to wear. I knew it was silly. We were just going to the movies and I could have been the third or even fourth person he'd asked to take his cousin's ticket. But what if I wasn't? What if Nick liked me? I'd been trying NOT to like him ever since the first day I'd met him. Because that would not be smart. At least, that's what I told myself. Still, there were a lot of good things about Nick to like. He was kind and cute, just like Wilma said. He didn't brag or try to act tough. He also didn't shrink away from challenges. Nick said he wanted to get a PhD someday, and I believed he would.

Maybe I do like him? No. I can't. But maybe. I don't know. Don't think about it, Rayna.

I finally settled on my black jeans, black-and-white Jack the Pumpkin King T-shirt, and an oversize red-and-black plaid shirt. All that was left to choose were the shoes.

I looked around the edges of my room, where I had my custom sneakers lined up on display and considered my options. It never took me this long to pick out an outfit. *Just pick already!* Eventually, I settled on my oldest pair, my most trusted pair, the ones I always wore when I had to be extra courageous—the black ones with little white skulls I'd worn on my first day at FMS.

Finally, I was ready, and just in time. As I was tying my laces, the doorbell rang, and I heard voices greeting each other in the entryway. *Here goes nothing,* I thought as I went out to meet Nick's family.

By the time I got to the kitchen, there was a crowd around the breakfast bar. Aunty Jacq put some cookies in a tin as my mom and Mrs. Smallwood laughed at something Mr. Smallwood was saying. Nick peered sheepishly in my direction, nodding at the adults and shrugging his shoulders. I couldn't tell what was so funny either.

"I ran straight out of the head like my butt was on fire," Mr. Smallwood said, laughing even more.

"That prank was legendary!" Mom said. "No one could top Private Burchardt. He was a genius."

"Here she is," Aunty Jacq said, seeing me standing off to the side.

"I hope you are a Marvel lover," Mr. Smallwood said. "We're kind of superfans."

Even if he hadn't mentioned it, I'd have been able to tell. They all had enough swag on that they'd fit right in at Comic-Con.

"Absolutely," I said.

Mrs. Smallwood looked at her watch. "Ooooh, we better get going. You all ready?"

"Ready!" we chimed in. Aunty Jacq gave the tin of cookies to Mrs. Smallwood, who followed Nick's dad toward the car. Nick and I lagged slightly behind.

"I'm glad you're coming," Nick told me.

My cheeks turned hot. "Me too," I said.

"Dad tells the truth. We kind of go all in on Marvel movies."

"I can see that," I said, pointing at Nick's shirt with a STARK INDUSTRIES insignia on it.

"Heck yeah!" he said smiling. "Smarts, big smarts. Big inventions. Sometimes stupid decisions."

I chuckled and followed him out to their car.

I've always thought that Black Widow was the coolest character in all the Marvel Universe, and this movie was not changing my mind. Loki was funny, the Hulk was amazing, but Black Widow was my hero. She had a hard time letting people in, but still cared about others. I got that.

I bet Wilma did, too. When I saw how sad she and her dad were together, it reminded me that I was lucky to be blessed with the family I had. Maybe it was just me, my mom, and my aunt, and maybe I hated moving all the time and worrying about my mom, but there were other people having a hard time, too. So even though I didn't have a dog or a huge group of best friends, I decided I'd try to be more like Black Widow and help where I could.

I wondered about Nick and his family, too. What challenges they had. Outside of serving the vets food on Thanksgiving, I'd never had Native friends or been to any Native person's house. At least, I didn't think I had. Mr. Smallwood looked like a lot of other dads I'd seen in the military. His hair was cut in the short, military fashion. He had dark skin and the same turquoise eyes as Nick, but I wouldn't have known he was Cherokee if Nick hadn't told me. Nick's mom had lighter skin and deep brown eyes. I bet most people thought she was White.

On Thanksgiving, Nick had talked about how most Native people felt invisible. Maybe that was my fault, too. Especially if I was always expecting them to look like the characters I saw in movies, like Tiger Lily in *Peter Pan*.

"The movie's amazing, right?" Nick asked, leaning toward me. His face was so close to mine. Goose bumps shot up all over me.

"Yeah," I whispered back, not looking at him. No way could I look at him. Then he'd *know*.

"Who's your favorite? Thor?"

I guffawed. "Uh, no. Black Widow, thank you."

He smiled. "Yeah, she seems your style."

I felt a jolt from a few seats over. Mr. Smallwood was elbowing Nick. Popcorn flew out of Nick's bag. "I told you he'd get out," he said, pointing at the screen.

Nick chuckled at his dad, and so did I. He brushed the loose popcorn off his shirt and focused back on the movie.

All too soon, the heroes had saved the world and the movie was over.

On the way back to my house, Nick and his family discussed their favorite scenes, debated on what would happen in the next movie, and laughed—like a lot, and it was contagious.

"Thanks for going with me today," Nick said, walking me to my door. "And for putting up with my superfan family."

"They are amazing. Your dad is so funny," I said.

A honk interrupted us as we lingered for a minute on the front porch. "Hey, Nick, we'll be right back, okay?" Mrs. Smallwood called from the car window.

"What?" Nick shouted. "Why?"

Nick's mom gave him a giant smile. "We're going to gas up the car while you two say goodbye."

"Um . . . okay." Nick gave me a curious look and shrugged his shoulders as his parents drove off. "So . . . I guess I've been left here?"

"Looks like it," I said. "There is a gas station literally two streets away on the main road, so they'll be back soon."

We sat down on the porch steps.

Nick shivered in the cool winter breeze. "This is a really

nice street. Sure beats the houses on the bases, right?"

"Oh yeah," I said. "It's the nicest place we've ever lived in. And my aunty Jacq is really loving the town. The farmers' markets, the bookstores and restaurants downtown, the amazing ice cream shops."

"Have you been to the store that sells just soda? Like any kind of flavor you've ever seen?" he asked.

"Not yet, but that is definitely going on my to-do list." I grinned.

"I remember when we first moved here. It was so weird. I just wasn't used to *staying* anywhere."

I stiffened, nervous about where the conversation was going. I didn't like to talk about moving, but if anyone were to get it, it would be Nick, so I tried to relax.

"It took me a little while to feel comfortable around people," he continued.

"You?" I had a hard time believing that.

"Yep. I just wasn't used to making friends outside of tribal events or hanging out with cousins."

The wind was picking up, pushing and pulling the bare tree limbs around in a frenzy. I shoved my hands farther into my pockets. "I want to have friends here, but . . ."

"You don't know how long you'll be here, right?"

"Yeah," I said.

We sat there quietly for a while. I knew he got it. We both understood how easy it was for your life to change in an instant. How tired it could make you.

The sound of tires approaching broke our silence. Nick's parents were back. We stood and waited for the car to pull up in front of my house.

"You were right. That was fast," Nick said. If I wasn't mistaken, he sounded disappointed.

I looked down at my shoes and summoned all my courage to look him right in the eyes. "Thanks for inviting me today, Nick."

"There wasn't anyone else I'd rather have gone with," he said.

We stood there awkwardly for a few seconds longer.

"Bye, Rayna Snow," he said. Then he turned and made his way back down my porch steps.

"Bye, Nick Smallwood," I whispered. As I watched him walk away, the chilly wind nipped at my skin. But inside I was floating on a cloud—a Rayna-shaped cloud of happy, dancing skulls.

27

Once inside, the first thing I heard was Aunty Jacq and Mom discussing something in serious voices. I hovered outside the kitchen.

"When would the change happen?" Aunty Jacq asked.

"In a couple of months if I agree," Mom replied.

Were they talking about reassignment? My whole body began to shake. Nick and I were just . . . *Not again. Not again.*

"I thought you were considering a civilian job?" Aunty Jacq asked.

"I was. I am," Mom said. "But if I re-up for another year or so, I'll definitely be promoted. It'd be better for us financially if I leave at a higher station."

"But . . . ?" Aunty Jacq asked tentatively.

"The promotion would mean spending a lot more time in Asia. That's why I've been going to San Diego. To observe the person in the position now."

I heard Aunty Jacq sigh. "Rayna and I are used to the drill. But she's twelve now. She's growing up fast, Kate. I'm afraid you'll miss out on some of her most important years, and you may regret it. Would this mean you'd be stationed in California?" Aunty Jacq asked.

Now my mom sighed. "I just keep thinking about getting her college paid for," she said, not answering the question.

I couldn't listen anymore. I was furious, hurt, disgusted. I ran to my bedroom and slammed the door.

Aunty Jacq must have heard me. "Rayna, is that you?" she called out.

"Yes!" I said as cheerfully as possible so they wouldn't come in and talk to me. I wanted to be left alone. Seriously alone.

Spike was awake. As he wandered about in his cage, tears rolled freely down my face. "Hey, Spike," I said, choking on my words. "How you doing, buddy?" I opened up the top of the cage and pulled him out. I couldn't catch my breath.

I lay down on the bed and dropped Spike on my chest, trying not to think about Nick and Wilma. Aunty Jacq's promises. How I'd never be normal. Never live in a normal place. With a normal life. And normal friends. I'd always be the girl that left.

"It's just you and me, buddy," I whispered. "Just you and me."

Spike crawled closer to me and sniffed my whole face, leaving no spot unloved. All I could do was cry.

28

Frederick Middle School was decoration-free. It seemed odd that for the past week, the halls hadn't been bathed in one color or another. Instead, they had a sterilized feeling and smelled of bleach and cleaning products, like a hospital. Even my locker looked shiny, as if it had been wiped down and polished. It was also very cold out. Snow had blanketed the school grounds and filled in the corners of the windows.

And for once, I wasn't the only one who was quiet. I guess no one liked being back from winter break. Looking around the almost-silent hallways, everyone—the students *and* the teachers—looked glum.

Nick and I were friendly with each other in class, but I kept myself busy and tried to appear as studious as possible. I needed time and distance if we were going to leave. I couldn't allow myself to get any closer to him than I already had. It would hurt too much when I had to say goodbye.

Marcie, Kevin, and Matt had all said their regular hellos to me in the halls and on the bus. I'd said hello back, but that was about it. And it felt normal, whatever normal was supposed to feel like.

I didn't know what to do about Wilma. I hadn't seen her at all between Christmas and New Year's Day, and had spent the afternoons training Spike all by myself. I'd been a little worried about her, but I figured she and her dad had things to work out.

Plus, I had my own worries to deal with. I'd been preparing myself for "the talk" I'd get from Aunty Jacq and my mom. And leaving FMS.

On our first day back, I'd been scared to see Wilma because I wasn't looking forward to telling her what I'd heard Mom and Aunty Jacq saying. But all those thoughts had quickly flown from my head when I saw her climb onto the bus. She barely wore any makeup, which wasn't like her at all. And after giving me a small wave, she sat across the aisle, pulled her hoodie over her head, and conked out against the window.

The whole week had passed by like that. Wilma slept on the bus and disappeared into the crowd at school. Nick and I chatted in Mr. Toliver's class, but I kept a low profile. The week was like one long, cold, sterile day.

Now Friday had arrived. Language arts was my last class, and while I waited for my teacher to grade our quizzes and hand them back, I read a chapter from *Ninth Ward* and tried not to count the seconds until the bell rang.

But I was having a hard time concentrating on the book in front of me. I actually liked it a lot. It was about a girl in the Ninth Ward of New Orleans right before Hurricane Katrina struck the shore, and the worry everyone felt waiting for the storm to hit. I'd just gotten to the part where the main character was preparing for landfall, and I really wanted to see if she was going to make it, but no luck—worries filled my thoughts, and I stared at the same page forever.

All of a sudden a paper was placed on my desk, bringing me back to attention. It was my quiz. I turned it over to see that I'd gotten a B+. *B-plus?!* I screamed inside. I read through the quiz, searching for what I did wrong. I had totally missed the second part of a question.

Yep. I was losing, failing. All the rules I'd set for myself, my goals for the school year, were all slipping away. *Get a dog? Fail. Avoid making friends. Fail. Get all As in school. Fail, fail, fail.*

The bell couldn't ring soon enough. I wanted to get away from FMS as quickly as I could. *This is such a stupid school,* I told myself. FMS wasn't special. Every school was the same. *So what if I made a B-plus. So what if I leave. Who cares about this stupid, stupid town and this stupid, stupid school and this stupid, stupid grade!*

Rinnggg!

I grabbed my book bag and shoved the terrible quiz into its depths, not caring if it got all crumpled up, and ran out of the room.

"Hey," Nick said, surprising me in the hallway. "Hold up."

"Um, hey," I said, looking at him briefly as I tried to get my bag situated on my back.

"I was wondering—" he began.

"Sorry," I said, cutting him off. "I'm so sorry to interrupt you. I just have to run, um, I don't mean to be rude—"

"Totally fine," he said. "You're in a hurry. See you next week?"

"Yeah, sure, I mean, yes. Of course. Um. Thank you."
Courteous half smile.

I couldn't believe I'd just given Nick that smile. The smile for strangers. I headed quickly toward my locker, turning back just for a second to see Nick's face, watching me as I went.

He knew what I was doing. And I knew he knew.

29

Saturday-morning light shone through my windows. The snow must have ended, and the gray skies cleared. I could hear Aunty Jacq bustling around in the kitchen. Saturday pancakes.

I felt happy for a second and then sad thinking about Aunty Jacq, who was doing what she called "blooming" in Frederick. Her paintings were particularly beautiful, full of places you wanted to go and just *be*. Some were imaginary, some were based on real life. But no matter what they were, they always had a homey feeling to them. I wanted that for her . . . for us . . . in the real.

I rolled over in bed, but didn't climb out just yet. I was too full of emotion. The odds that we'd be moving had begun to feel more likely, especially since Mom had gone back to San Diego . . . again. She was there for the next few weeks, and sometimes when she called at night, I pretended I was asleep so I didn't have to talk to her. She didn't care about me or Aunty Jacq. Not really. I always thought the army called all the shots, and that's who I should be mad at. But knowing that Mr. Smallwood had retired, and hearing Mom's conversation with Aunty Jacq, I knew that if we moved again, it would be all her fault. Her fault completely.

My phone buzzed. I reached over and picked it up from my nightstand. I didn't recognize the number, so I took a closer look.

> Cool hedgehog owner

> Wilma here

> My dad gave me my phone back

> And Nick gave me your #

> Is it ok 2 text?

Wilma sounded okay. I smiled. I was about to text back, but then I stopped myself. She'd been pretty distant over the past week, looking like she hadn't wanted to be bothered with other people's feelings—the same as me. A dangerous thought passed through my mind. *If I don't text her back—like ever—will she just move on? Forget all about me? Maybe that would be best.*

I bolted upright in bed. *What am I thinking?!* I could never ghost Wilma like I'd been ghosted. I knew that when I told her about what was happening with my mom, she would be way nicer than my so-called friends in Pensacola.

Sure, Nose ring girl

Glad u got Ur phone back

When does Hedgie Gym start again?

My stomach wrapped itself up like a tight piece of tortellini. A part of me really didn't want to hang out with anyone. I'd rather just lie in bed forever and never leave my room again. I didn't want to be rude or make Wilma feel bad, but I needed some time alone so I'd be ready to say goodbye.

Not sure

He comes when I call him

Maybe that's good enough?

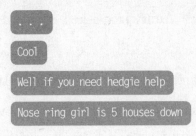

Cool

Well if you need hedgie help

Nose ring girl is 5 houses down

Thx ☺

I promised myself that I'd talk to Wilma, tell her everything. As soon as I could.

The smell of pancakes filled the house. My gloom and doom weren't strong enough to keep me from them. The weekend tradition was something that made sense, something I could hold on to. I threw the covers back and grabbed my usual fuzzy socks and hoodie.

"There she is. How did you sleep, Angel?" Aunty Jacq asked as I sat up at the breakfast bar.

"Meh," I said.

"Well, maybe these will help." She slid a plate of beautiful golden pancakes under my nose. There was a large spoonful of whipped cream tucked into them on one side. "Lemon," she said, proud of her work.

I took a bite. They were like a fluffy hug on a plate. I began to cry.

"Oh, Angel, are you okay?" Aunty Jacq asked, sitting down next to me and rubbing my back.

I gathered myself together and wiped my eyes. "I'm sorry, Aunty Jacq, I'm just . . ." I couldn't finish. I didn't even know how to say what I was feeling. "These are really delicious. And I'm really grateful."

"You're welcome, Angel."

I took a few more bites while Aunty Jacq got up to pour herself another cup of coffee.

"Is it okay if I don't want to talk to Mom when she calls tonight?" I asked hesitantly.

"Did you two have an argument I don't know about?"

"No, it's just . . . never mind. It's okay." I couldn't tell her how I was feeling. If I did, she'd know I overheard her and Mom's conversation.

Aunty Jacq came back and sat next to me. "Come here, you," she said, pulling me into a hug and then holding me away from her to look me in the eye. "I'm right here, okay? You let me know if you need to talk about something. Anything."

I nodded and gave her a small smile. "Thanks, Aunty Jacq."

I spent the rest of the day sitting in my room training Spike and thinking. I made a tiny, makeshift Hedgie Gym on my bed out of books placed in a square in the center of the bed. Then I practiced holding out a worm on the end of the tweezers and beckoning my hedgie.

"Spike, come over here," I called. He waddled over to me and ate the worm. "Okay, Spike, roll over."

Spike walked over to the tweezers, sniffing up toward the worm I held at the ready. "Roll over, Spike." I used my other hand to pick him up and put him on his back. "Roll over like this."

Spike wrapped himself into a chunky little spiked ball, then popped his head out.

"I get it," I said. "You're not ready." I fed him the worm anyway and then moved the books over so I could lie down on my bed. Holding a fuzzy pillow over my heart, I took a deep breath. "I'm not ready either."

30

It was official. Nick definitely thought I'd blown him off because I was moving. Another two weeks had come and gone at school, and I'd managed to feign being too busy to hang out. Yesterday in class, he'd given me his easy smile from across the room. But he'd seemed hurt, too. At one point, I glanced up to find him looking at me with a concerned expression on his face. He quickly looked away, but I glued my eyes back on my book, in case he looked over at me again.

Marcie, Kevin, and Matt hadn't made any surprise visits to my house either. I listened to them on the bus like I always did. Mostly the discussions were about the upcoming science fair—which seemed to have their full attention. Kevin and Matt were doing separate experiments thanks to their mom, who'd asked their science teacher to separate them. Kevin's experiment was on the different methods of dating rocks, and Matt's was on the formation of sparkly geodes. Marcie deflected every question the boys asked about her experiment. She wasn't telling them *anything*.

They'd only asked me once about Spike and how things were going with his training. My answer? "Good, thanks for asking." And that was it.

Then there was Wilma. She'd always sleep in the mornings on the bus, and then we'd talk about nothing much on the trip home. A couple of times after getting off the bus, she'd linger on the sidewalk in front of my house to see if I'd invite her in. I kept things friendly and acted like nothing was wrong, but I never asked her over. I kept promising myself that I'd tell her what was going on, but I was chicken. Chicken with a capital *C*. Would she really be cool? I hated myself for being cagey. Every week I felt more like a loser.

Now there I was, on another Friday, dreading when we'd get off the bus because I knew I wouldn't invite her over—again.

"TGIF. I can't take being at the school for another second.

The walls are bleeding with Pepto-Bismol," she said as we got settled on the bus.

I rolled my eyes. "They really are. I've never seen a school so covered in red and pink in my life."

"What's the point of Valentine's Day? I mean, really?" she asked.

"I have no idea. Aren't all saints martyrs, and don't they die horrible deaths?"

"Let's look," she said, searching for something on her smartphone. "Saint Valentine's also the patron saint of bookkeepers and epilepsy."

I couldn't help but chuckle. "Random."

"He watches over engaged couples, marriages, traveling, *and* keeps you from getting the plague and fainting."

The bus pulled up to the stop at the end of our street. I yanked my slouchy winter hat farther down on my ears and grabbed my backpack. After everyone had passed me off the bus, I slid out of the seat and hopped off. Wilma was right behind me. We walked down our street, shivering.

"It's so cold," she said. She only had on a hoodie with a denim jacket over it.

I was warmer in a black coat with a hood that I'd pulled up over my hat. "Fake fur," I said, pointing at my hood. "It's the best."

As we neared my house, my mind searched for something to say so that I wouldn't have to invite her in, so I wouldn't have to tell her my news. When we made it to the path that led up to my house, all I'd come up with was "Maybe see you this weekend?" It was not really an invite, but it put off talking about it.

"Sure," Wilma said, but her eyes looked at me suspiciously. Like she knew I wouldn't be texting her. "Rayna, are you okay?" she asked.

"Yeah, sure, I mean . . ."

"You know you can tell me if something's going on."

"Of course!" I said, brushing off her sincerity and feeling terrible for it.

"You and Nick haven't been hanging as much either," she said.

How does she know that? I became more and more nervous.

"Rayna," she said, expectantly, waiting for me to spill.

"We'll hang, okay? I've just got . . . I mean . . . we're good, right?"

"Yes," she said flatly, seeing right through me. I knew that she knew I didn't want to hang out.

"Cool," I said, turning to stare at my front porch, where we'd first met and had our first real conversation. I wanted to cry. But I couldn't. I wanted to tell her I wasn't pulling away because of her. That I really did want to hang out. That I was terrified. And making everything worse. But I couldn't help it.

As I turned back toward her, Wilma was already walking toward her house.

"See ya, nose ring girl."

Her hand went up to wave goodbye, but she didn't turn around.

It sucked. It sucked bad. I stormed up to the house, angry with myself. In my head, I started to make excuses. Maybe things were better this way. If she was mad at me or annoyed, it wouldn't hurt her when I left. That didn't make me feel any better, though. *Get over it, Rayna,* I told myself. But I felt angry. Angry I couldn't just be normal. Make friends and keep them like other kids did. And it was all my mom's fault. There was no way I'd be talking to her on the phone tonight. *Forget it.*

After dinner, I sat at my desk, working on two new pairs of Converse. They were the fiercest, ugliest, blackest, darkest, angriest shoes I'd ever painted. Angry skeletons bathed in fire leapt from one pair, and a black heart with creepy green veins oozed over the sides of the second pair. As I was working on the shading of the black hearts, I tried to think about whether I should add some barbed wire around them, instead of all the things I didn't want to think about.

Since the lemon pancakes last Saturday, I'd also been on Aunty Jacq's radar. She'd been checking in on me more often and hanging out with me and Spike. But I hadn't felt like talking to anyone but Spike. I'd begun putting him in his carrying pouch and strapping him around my chest while I painted.

Justin had been right. It had taken a while, but Spike came to me when I called him. He'd gotten pretty pudgy. Worms were definitely hedgie junk food.

There was a knock on my door.

"Come in," I said.

"Your mom's on the phone," Aunty Jacq said, gliding into the room. "I think you should talk to her, at least a few minutes, okay?" She sat down next to me and handed me her cell phone before I had a chance to refuse.

"Hey, Mom," I said, putting her on speaker and continuing to paint.

"Hi, Angel, how are you? How was your Friday?"

"Fine," I said.

"How is Spike?" she asked. "Jacq says he's learned how to come to you when you call him."

"Yes," I said.

Silence hung between us on the call.

"Rayna, what's going on?" she finally asked.

"Nothing, Mom, I was just painting when you called."

"Listen, when I get back—" she began.

"When will that be?" I interrupted, holding my paintbrush midair, waiting on her answer.

"Well, I'm not—"

"Right, it's the army's call."

"Listen, Rayna, you're obviously not yourself tonight." I rolled my eyes. "But I love you, and I'll call you tomorrow."

"Okay." I picked up the phone and handed it back to Aunty Jacq.

"Hi, Kate . . . yeah . . . okay. No, it's okay . . . Sure. G'night."

I waited for Aunty Jacq to get up and leave the room now that the call was over, but she didn't. "You got a second, Angel?" she asked.

Okay. This seems serious.

I plopped my paintbrush into the water jar and turned fully around in my desk chair to face her.

"Sure," I said. *Here it comes. Some kind of excuse from my mom.*

"My showing is in two weeks, can you believe it? I feel like it was just Christmas."

"That's great, Aunty Jacq," I said, looking at her expectantly. *Is she not going to talk to me about my behavior?* "Do you need my help with something?"

"No, just wanted to talk about the night of."

"Okay," I said.

"Is there someone you would like to bring with you to the event?" she asked, beaming. "Maybe Wilma or Nick? He's awfully nice, that Nick."

"No," I said, tensing up and becoming a little defensive. Spike stuck his head up out of his pouch and wiggled his nose in Aunty Jacq's direction. I unstrapped his carrying pouch and set it on the bed next to her. The hedgie began to run around and sniff everything he could get his nose on. At least one of us was having a good time.

"Are you sure? After you help me set up that night, I may

be talking to a lot of people, and I don't want you just sitting somewhere bored."

"I really don't want to ask anyone. I'm fine being alone," I said, not wanting the conversation to go much further.

Aunty Jacq looked down at Spike, who was sniffing at her elbow. "Rayna, I know you're not okay. You've stopped seeing any of your new friends or really talking to anyone. What's going on, Angel?" she asked gently, looking up at me with real concern in her eyes.

"Why don't YOU tell ME what's going on?" My voice was going up in decibels. I felt as mean as my new shoes looked. "Or why doesn't Mom tell me what's going on? Are we moving to San Diego or what?"

Aunty Jacq's voice was calm. "Is that what you're worried about?"

"Shouldn't I be? We just got here. And now Mom is ready to up and go somewhere else?"

"She can't tell them where she wants to be," Aunty Jacq said.

"Oh, no? But she could retire, right?" I said accusingly.

Aunty Jacq sighed. "Did you hear us talking about that?" I ignored the question. "No one knows what's going to happen yet. Your mom's got a lot to think about, and I know it doesn't seem like it, but she really is trying to decide what's best for you and for her—"

"And what about you, Aunty Jacq," I interrupted. "Don't you like it here? Don't you want to stay? She can't even see what it's like for us to give up things anymore. She can't see anyone but herself. Not you, not me. It's not fair! She doesn't care. If she did, she'd listen to you, right? She only seems to care about the army and her rank. Why am I so invisible? Why are we invisible?"

I looked down at Spike. "I mean, like with a pet. Did she listen to what I wanted? No." My voice was shaking. "I asked for a dog. She's always heard me say that I wanted a dog. Dog. Dog. Dog. But she ignored it. Instead of a dog, what do I get? A hedgehog. A silly, stupid hedgehog. It's not the same. They don't shake your hand, go on walks, become your best friend. They don't do tricks." All my anger was shifting and piling up. I pointed at Spike sitting there on the bed. "Seriously! If you tell a hedgehog to roll over, it'll never ROLL OVER!"

Spike rolled over.

Aunty Jacq put her hand up over her mouth and looked at me. "Did he just . . ."

I was shocked. My anger popped like a balloon, leaving me

nothing but surprise. I quickly grabbed the can of worms sitting on my desk, opened it, and with my bare fingers reached in for a reward.

"Here you go, Spike," I said, handing it to him. He munched it happily. "Okay, boy," I said, hoping and praying this wasn't a fluke, "roll over."

Spike rolled over.

"This is fabulous!" Aunty Jacq exclaimed. I gave Spike another worm. He ran around on the bed, as cute as could be.

I wasn't thinking. I was so excited. I had to tell someone. I grabbed my dumb phone and found Nick's number.

> Ur not the only 1 with training skills

> My hedgehog can now roll over on command

Awesome!

> Thx

Did it just happen?

> Yeah

> My aunt and I were talking about her gallery show

> And I said roll over and he just did it

That's really cool

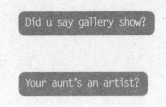

Did u say gallery show?

Yeah

Your aunt's an artist?

Yeah

I looked over at Aunty Jacq and Spike, proud of them both. Proud of my family.

Do you want to go?

2 the show?

Yeah

When is it?

All of a sudden, I realized what I was doing. *Oh my god.* I was about to ask Nick out for Valentine's Day. But what could I do? I couldn't take the invitation back now.

2/14

BRB

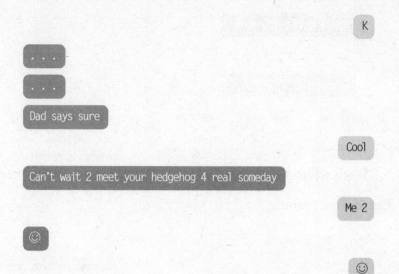

My face turned red. I'd been a serious jerk for weeks, and he was still being nice to me. Part of me was relieved, and the other part . . .

Oh my god. What did I just do?

31

The night of the show came quickly. The gallery sat along the canal that ran along the edge of Frederick's downtown area. It was just after dark, and the gallery's large glass walls meant I could look out onto the beautiful bridges strung with twinkling lights crisscrossing the canal and the water lilies, miraculously still green, drifting on top of the water. It was downright magical.

I was so proud of my aunty Jacq. People crowded around her paintings and praised them with all kinds of amazing compliments. Plus, outside of wearing her favorite apron in the kitchen, this was the first time in a long time that I had seen my aunty Jacq really fit in somewhere. I remembered how she had promised me that no matter what, we'd be at the gallery show together. And here we were.

Nick texted me saying he'd be there in ten minutes. I was nervous to see him. I mean, I had seen him in school, but he'd let me keep my distance, let me have my space. That made me like him even more, and I really didn't know what to do about that.

"Rayna."

I turned to see Nick smiling his amazing smile and walking toward me from across the room. He was dressed nicer than I had ever seen him, wearing jeans, checkered Vans, a red T-shirt, and a black jacket. And he was wearing earrings—small copper coins that hung just below his earlobes. I had no idea he had pierced ears. His hair was pulled neatly back into one long braid. He looked older to me. I knew I was staring, but I couldn't stop.

"Hey," he said, when he finally reached me.

"Hey," I said, all other words leaving me.

"You look really nice," he said. I looked down at the red-and-black checked skirt and fuzzy, black sweater that Aunty Jacq had helped me pick out.

"Thanks," I said. "Um, so do you."

"Thanks."

"Want to walk around and see the art?"

"That's usually what folks do at art shows," he said, teasing.

"Yep."

I first took him over to see Aunty Jacq's paintings. He was really impressed, looking at each one very thoughtfully. "Her paintings make me want to smile and cry at the same time."

"Same," I said, looking at one of my favorites. In it, jasmine grew in through an open window, and on a table under it, an opened letter. The envelope read, *I'm sorry.*

"Do you ever ask her what they mean?" he asked.

"Sometimes. But sometimes I just see my aunty Jacq in them. Like this one. She taught me to always bring tea or cocoa with an apology—something to share."

Nick looked at the painting, taking it in. "So maybe the jasmine is like tea," he said.

"Maybe," I said. "Or maybe it means something only Aunty Jacq knows."

Nick grinned. "Well, I love it."

"Me too." I grinned back.

After looking at Aunty Jacq's paintings, we walked around,

looking at the other artists' work, making comments here and there. Laughing a lot. Sometimes we just stood quietly, looking at a piece together.

At one point we went to the bar and got two sodas. Aunty Jacq was talking to a very well-dressed man wearing a wool scarf. She spotted Nick and me out of the corner of her eye and gave us a wave and a smile.

"You want to sit down for a sec over there?" Nick asked, pointing at a carved wooden bench up against a wall.

"Lead the way," I said. Soon we were sitting side by side and looking out into the crowd.

"Rayna, can I ask you something personal? You don't have to answer. But I've been thinking about you lately."

He's thinking about me?

"Is your mom getting reassigned?"

My heart dropped out of my chest, and my arms ran cold.

"It's just, you haven't really wanted to talk or hang out, and that's how I used to get every time we were about to move."

"I don't know," I said truthfully. "I overheard my mom telling Aunty Jacq that she's thinking of re-upping for another year so she can get promoted."

Nick looked at me with genuine understanding.

"I heard her say she's been observing someone in that position in San Diego. I think if she says yes, she'll be in Asia a lot, and we'll have to move to California."

"I'm sorry, Rayna. When will you find out for sure?"

I shrugged. "Could be tomorrow, next month?"

"Listen, I know that everyone always says they'll write or they'll stay in touch when your parents get reassigned, and I know that almost never happens. But I promise that won't happen with me, okay?"

I couldn't take it. Why did he have to say that? Even if Nick really did believe that he would text or call or whatever, I knew that was probably never going to happen. That just wasn't how things worked.

"You can't promise that," I said briskly.

"I can promise to try. How about we try?"

Terror ran through me. The gallery disappeared. Suddenly, I was in Pensacola, checking my phone over and over for messages that never came. Waiting for my friends to talk to me again. Driving away with no one waving goodbye. I thought my heart was going to break in my chest. "Um . . . I think I should . . . um. I'm going to go to the restroom, okay?"

"Yeah, sure. Listen, I'm sorry to bring it up."

"We're good." Courteous half smile. *Dang it, Rayna! Don't do this to Nick!*

I ran to the restroom and slammed into a stall, trying to breathe. Panic ran through me. *Why does this have to keep happening?* I didn't know why I was so mad. Nick was genuine, the real deal, and I knew it. But I couldn't count on that. It would hurt too much when I stopped hearing from him. What had I been thinking? Why did I ever think I could make a friend in this stupid town!

I banged the side of the stall with my fist and sucked in a huge gasp of air. Then I cried. I cried for what seemed like forever.

Sitting on the edge of the toilet seat with my head in my hands, I stared at the zigzag pattern of floor tiles, which seemed to swim in front of my eyes.

There was no way I could go back out there. I leaned up against the stall walls, listening to toilets flushing and sinks running. But I couldn't move.

I don't know how long I sat there. Maybe thirty minutes.

Maybe an hour. Eventually, I heard a soft knock on the stall door.

"Rayna, Angel, are you in there?"

Silence.

"The gallery show is over, and they're closing up for the night. It's time to go home, okay?"

Without any other choice, I stood up, unlocked, and opened the door. When I saw Aunty Jacq's worried expression, I ran into her arms.

"It's okay, Angel. It's okay. Let's go home now, all right?"

I nodded, tears running down my face as I held her tight.

She let me go and took my face into her hands. She wiped my cheeks and gently smoothed my hair.

"I'm sorry I ruined your show," I said, feeling selfish and horrible.

"You didn't ruin a thing, Angel. Not at all. You ready?"

I nodded.

Outside the bathroom, I caught a glimpse of Nick climbing into his dad's car through the gallery windows without a backward glance.

I don't blame him, I thought. I didn't deserve a goodbye.

32

I planned on staying in my pajamas all day. The night before had been so messed up. I had really treated Nick poorly, abandoning him at Aunty Jacq's show. I hadn't meant to hurt him, but I was sure that I had. Aunty Jacq had told me she'd talked to Nick and Mr. Smallwood before they left, and everything was okay. But it didn't feel like that. Nothing felt okay.

I cuddled up with Spike in his little carrying pouch and pulled the covers up around us both. The day was windy but sunny. I had raised the shades so that I could lie in bed peacefully and stare at the sky.

That morning Aunty Jacq had come in to check on me,

telling me I could eat my pancakes for dinner if I wanted. She brought me a big glass of water and let me sleep.

At the moment, Spike was the one who was fast asleep. I loved his steady breathing, and the way he would twitch every once in a while, probably dreaming of tasty worms and the running wheel he loved so much. I felt calmer when we hung out. Less like the world kept breaking over and over again.

Mom had come home in the wee hours of the morning. She'd missed Aunty Jacq's gallery show by a day. I knew she'd sleep awhile and I was glad for that. Of course, I was going to have to talk to her eventually. But not yet.

It wouldn't be long before the pet talent show at the VFW. I had promised my mom I'd do it. Told Marcie, Kevin, and Matt I'd do it. But with all that was happening, I didn't want to face anybody. Maybe, just maybe, Mom would let me out of it. She could make a few calls for me, tell everyone I was out.

Then again, backing out of the contest might mean that I failed Mom's "pet experiment," and I'd never get the dog she had been promising me.

I looked over at my alarm clock. It was ten thirty in the morning. Didn't care. Today would be a stay-in-bed day. A stay-away day.

My phone buzzed. I didn't want to look at it. But some-times my mom liked to text instead of yelling for me from the other end of the house, so I grabbed the phone and glanced at the screen.

It was Wilma. *Oh no.*

I pulled back my covers and rose from the bed. I felt shaky, scared. Tucking Spike and his pouch next to the pillows, I grabbed my hoodie and headed to the front door.

When I opened it, Wilma looked at me with a hard expression.

"What's going on?" I asked, genuinely concerned. I mean, I knew I'd been a jerk to her as well, but I also knew she had things going on at home. "Are you okay? Here," I said, opening the door wider, "do you want to come in?"

"I thought you'd be different," Wilma said. "The day you were out here, that barbecue day. I talked to you because you seemed real. You were honest."

"I'm sorry—"

"Don't," she said. "You were really nice to me on Christmas Eve, your family, too, and I won't forget that. But it's not cool to act like someone's friend one day and the next act like you can't wait for them to get out of your face."

I froze in the doorway. No words would come out of my mouth, even though I knew Wilma was right.

"Nick told me about how you left him alone at the gallery yesterday. Why'd you even invite him in the first place? He may be all forgiving and everything, but I say things like they are. Marcie, Kevin, and Matt can't figure out what they did to make you hate them."

"But I don't hate—"

"I just can't figure it out. Either something happened and you're *not* mad at anyone, or all the nice things you do are just fake. You said your friends quit talking to you when you had to move here, and that hurt? Well, maybe it was because they just didn't want to be around a fake person anymore."

That cut me to the core. "Wilma, it's not like that. Really. I'm not fake. Things are just . . ."

"Hard? Things are hard for everybody, Rayna."

And with that, Wilma shot like lightning off the porch and down the street.

I ran back to my room in tears. Everything was all my fault. Everything I was scared would happen was happening, and there wasn't anything I could do about it.

33

My plans to stay in my room the rest of the day didn't happen. At three o'clock, Mom was up and about and wanted my help in the backyard. She'd said to put on something warm that could get dirty.

I procrastinated. I did NOT want to help her with her garden. But I also couldn't say no. You didn't tell Mom no. At least I could bring Spike with me.

The hedgie wiggled and sniffed as I placed him in the new carrying pouch I'd bought from Justin the weekend before. It was a red, fuzzy purse style, and seeing Spike's face through the little mesh panel on the front was so cute.

"Ready to spend some time outside?" I asked him. I grabbed an old pair of beat-up sneakers that I would NEVER be seen in outside the house, then headed to the backyard with Spike.

Outside, Mom was beaming. *Didn't she know I was not okay?* "Rayna, grab that broom there by the door and sweep the back patio, would you?"

I set Spike's bag on the lawn chair by the door. His nose pressed up against the mesh window, sniffing. I grabbed the broom and began to sweep, my conversation with Wilma that morning still fresh in my mind. Her words had stung. They'd replayed over and over until I wasn't sure what I thought. I hadn't been fake, had I? I just hadn't wanted to hurt anyone. Or to be hurt myself.

I swept the porch with all my might, like I hated every corner of it, stopping from time to time to watch my mom measure the length of one of the raised beds she'd made with retractable tape.

"You can stop shooting daggers at me from over there, Rayna. What's on your mind?"

Yep. I was angry. So angry I could spit. But when the words came out, they weren't jumbled by fury. They were exact and full of the cold, hard truth. "Is there a point to all this?"

"What do you mean?" Mom asked, incredulous.

"I mean, why do you even bother with this garden? Why do you even bother with me?"

"Excuse me?"

"Why aren't you retiring—or letting your time run out or whatever? Then you'd be home like Mr. Smallwood is. I don't get it." My voice rose. "Why are you putting Aunty Jacq through this? Why are you putting ME through it?"

"Rayna, calm down, Angel—"

"Don't call me that!" I yelled. "Don't try to act like everything is normal. You get to leave and come home whenever the army commands, but it never affects you. YOU don't lose anything!"

My hands flailed as I spoke. I'd already thrown the broom off to the side of the patio. I was over it. SO over it. "Just go ahead and say it, Mom. Tell me we're moving to San Diego, that it will be great and I'll love it there. Go ahead."

"Rayna, please. Calm down. Let's go inside and talk about this."

"No, thanks," I said. I grabbed Spike's pouch off the chair, ran back through the house to my room, and slammed my door.

I was so tired. So, so tired. I collapsed onto my bed, rolling over and curling up on my side, crying hot, angry tears into my pillow like when I was little.

When I'd calmed down, I got up to take Spike out of his new pouch and put him back in his cage so he could run around on his wheel. But when I reached the pouch, he wasn't there. And the flap was open.

"Spike?" I looked around my comforter and under the bed. "Spike?" I yelled again as I began tearing up my room, throwing shoes, clothes, and art supplies out of my way. But Spike wasn't anywhere. "No, no!" I yelled.

Aunty Jacq was in my room before I knew it, followed by my mom. "Rayna, what's going on? Calm down and talk to us," Mom said.

"It's Spike," I said, sobbing. "He's gone."

34

I couldn't believe I'd lost Spike. Had I forgotten to zip his new pouch all the way? Maybe he'd fallen out of the little bag while I was running or yelling. He could've been anywhere.

We searched for hours. Together, Aunty Jacq, Mom, and I combed the house and the backyard. But then it got dark. And cold. And windy. There was no way we'd find him now. I was more worried about the little guy than I'd ever been about anything before.

Every once in a while, I'd have to sit down and cry for a minute. Aunty Jacq tried to help me feel better. But that just made it worse. I deserved what was happening. I deserved to lose Spike.

After all the complaining I'd done about him. After how I had treated Nick and Wilma.

At seven thirty, we gave up. We didn't say it out loud. But that's what we did. I went to my room and thought about cleaning the mess up, but I couldn't muster any motivation. Not when Spike's cage looked so empty.

Aunty Jacq came in half an hour later. "Rayna, dinner's ready," she said, cracking open the door.

"Go away," I grumbled from my bed.

Soon I was asleep. I woke up a few times during the night, sweaty and scared. I dreamed of people pointing at me, laughing. Dreams where Aunty Jacq and Mom had disappeared, and I couldn't find my way to them. Dreams where the house was sucked up into a tornado. I'd never felt so left behind. I never felt so much like a leaver.

When I woke up on Sunday, all was quiet. I looked at my alarm clock. It was eleven in the morning. I had slept a really long time. I searched my room for my fluffy socks and my hoodie and put them on. But a quick glance in my long black mirror told me I was a mess. My hair stuck straight up in some places and lay flat in others. I didn't care. I felt as quiet as the house. Numb.

The kitchen was empty. Neither Mom nor Aunty Jacq were in their rooms. I heard the sliding door to the backyard open and shut, so I followed the noise, sliding the back door open and stepping outside in my sock feet.

Marcie, Kevin, and Matt were rooting around in the bushes and beds my mom had been working in the day before. Marcie looked up to see me standing there. "Guys, guys," she said. Matt and Kevin got up from where they were kneeling and faced me, too.

I then felt a tap on my shoulder. I turned to see Wilma, who no longer looked angry. "We'll find Spike, Rayna," she said.

"Don't worry, Rayna, we've got you," Marcie echoed.

"Absolutely," Matt and Kevin said at the same time.

I nodded at them, speechless. Were they really all there for me? Even though I'd iced them out?

Aunty Jacq appeared at the sliding door, took one look at my swollen, blotchy face and messy pajamas, and beckoned me back to the house. "There you are. Come back inside, Rayna." She led me to the breakfast bar. "You have to eat something, okay?" She slid over two pieces of buttered toast with honey and a cup of warm hot chocolate.

I picked up a piece of toast and took a small bite. The salty butter was a comfort. A few sips of the hot chocolate gave me a little more comfort. So I kept going, chewing and drinking slowly, carefully. My world was upside down. All I could do was let things be.

Then the doorbell rang.

"You stay here, Angel. I got it." She walked out of the kitchen, and a moment later I heard voices. "Looks like we have another volunteer," Aunty Jacq said as she returned with Nick. I reached up to my hair, but then decided it didn't matter.

"Wilma told me your hedgehog was missing."

"How . . . ?" I whispered.

"Your aunt called Matt and Kevin's mom to see if they would help look for him."

I glanced over at Aunty Jacq, who gave me a gentle smile.

"Then Matt and Kevin called Marcie. Marcie called Wilma, and Wilma called me."

Tears sprang to my eyes. I took in what Nick was saying, that even though I'd pushed them all away, they were helping me because they were kind. I felt so guilty. So embarrassed. I didn't deserve them. My body felt tired and weak.

"Thank you," I said quietly.

"We got you," he replied.

"Everyone else is out in the backyard," Aunty Jacq said. "It's right through the living room there." She pointed Nick toward the sliding door.

When he was out of earshot, I whispered, "Where's Mom?"

"She had to go to Fort Meade first thing," Aunty Jacq said. Why Mom would have to go there on a Sunday didn't make any sense to me. "But don't worry. She'll be back later on this afternoon."

"Aunty Jacq, I'm so tired."

"Eat a little bit more for me, okay?"

I took a few bites and drank the cocoa, then let Aunty Jacq help me back to my room, where I crawled into bed and shut my eyes. I was worried about Spike, but totally exhausted. Whatever happened, I accepted my fate.

35

"Rayna, wake up, honey." Aunty Jacq was sitting on the edge of my bed. "Have some water," she said, handing me a tall glass.

"What time is it?" I asked her as I sat up.

"Two."

I downed the whole glass of water in one long gulp. I must have been really thirsty.

"Jacq! Rayna!" I heard Kevin yell.

"Back here!" Aunty Jacq called to the other end of the house. I heard bounding feet heading in our direction.

Kevin and Matt burst in. "We found him!"

"You did?" Relief and excitement swept over me.

"Yeah," Matt said. "Spike's tucked in a hole under some tree roots in Mrs. Gomez's backyard, but he won't come out."

I stumbled out of bed, grabbing the closest pair of Converse and shoving my feet into them, and followed Matt and Kevin into the backyard, and out the side gate to Mrs. Gomez's yard.

Marcie was waiting at the gate. "He's over here, Rayna, come quick."

I followed her over to a tall oak tree. Nick and Wilma were crouched down by its base, but when they spotted me, they got up so I could take their place. I knelt down to find Spike's little behind sticking out from under one of the tree's roots. He was curled up in a tight little ball. I reached for the little hedgie, worries crashing through my mind. *What if Spike runs away? What if he doesn't know who I am?*

I gently brushed his back with my hand. "Hey, Spike. Let's go home, buddy, okay?"

Spike stuck his head out and turned an ear toward me to listen.

"It's me, Rayna. Come on, buddy, let's go."

Spike sniffed at the air and then uncurled himself completely. *Please don't run away,* I pleaded silently.

Spike sniffed the air again and then quickly ran into my hands, crawling up my arm, then into my hair. I was beyond happy. Wiping the tears off my cheeks, I stood as the rescue party surrounded me, cheering.

"You did it, Rayna!" Marcie said.

I looked at every one of their faces, so happy and kind.

"We did it," I said. "All of us."

36

The next day, I had a lot of messes to clean up. Not just my room, but with my friends. Yeah, I accepted it. I had friends. I had been so terrible to everyone, and they had still been so kind to me. Kind with a capital *K*. It was time to make tea—or maybe Aunty Jacq's shortbreads—and apologize.

When the search and rescue mission was complete, Wilma, Marcie, Matt, and Kevin had agreed to come back after school the next day for a thank-you treat. Nick had to do his sixth-grade tutoring after school, but he'd given me a giant hug and told me we could definitely hang out later in the week.

Aunty Jacq called FMS to let them know I would be out.

I'd told her that I could still go to school, but she'd said, "No, Angel. You've had a lot going on. This is what adults call taking a personal day. You need it."

So after breakfast, I began the first task: cleaning my room. I put away my shoes, changed the sheets, cleaned out Spike's cage. He was taking a personal day, too. There would be no Hedgie Gym today.

Right before lunch there was a knock at the front door. I heard Aunty Jacq greet someone and say, "She's in her room. Go on in."

A few moments later, Wilma stood in my doorway. "Hey, girl with a hedgehog, can I come in?"

I smiled. "Yes you can, girl with a nose ring."

"Why aren't you at school today?" I asked, sitting down on my bed.

Wilma peered into Spike's cage, then sat in my desk chair and swiveled toward me. "Shots," she said.

"Shots?" I asked.

"Yeah, I was due for a vaccine. My dad said I could take the rest of the day off."

"Sweet," I said, looking at my shoes. "Um, Wilma . . ."

"Rayna."

"I'm really sorry. On Christmas Day, after I went to the movies with Nick, I overheard my mom telling Aunty Jacq that she might stay in the military longer, and that we'd have to move to San Diego. I freaked out. I didn't want to have any friends, because I thought I'd just lose them. And if I could just keep everyone away, no one would get hurt. I'm sorry I was fake and not honest."

"You're not fake, Rayna, just . . . scared."

"Still, I'm sorry," I said.

"Apology accepted!" she said, grinning. Then her expression grew serious. "You know, when I lost my mom, all I ever wanted was to have more time with her. She just disappeared from my life. Afterward, I'd cry at stupid things. Like if I saw someone wearing a Columbia University T-shirt, I'd lose it because she'd gone to school there and had all these T-shirts she'd never let us put in the dryer. She would hang them all over the house to dry. My dad and I had thought it was SO annoying. But now I miss it. I still have a few of them. And I still hang them to dry. Anyway, I guess what I mean is that any amount of time you have with the people you care about is special."

I nodded. "I think I'm finally getting that."

"Rayna!" Aunty Jacq stuck her head inside the room. "Are you two hungry? I have some lunch in the kitchen, if you'd like."

"Uh, yeah!" Wilma said, and quickly followed Aunty Jacq from the room.

Wilma was a food lover. Another reason we were destined to be friends.

Later that afternoon, Marcie, Kevin, and Matt gathered around my kitchen island like they had that first day at the barbecue. Wilma had already gone home, but she'd told me she'd see me on the bus in the morning. I set the plate of shortbreads down on the kitchen island and cleared my throat. "Um, guys, I owe you an apology."

Marcie stood up tall, beaming.

"I think you are the smartest people I've ever met. I'm sorry that I avoided you all the time. Um . . ." I took a breath. "It's kind of hard for me to make friends when I have to move around a lot. I push people away 'cause I'm scared. But, that wasn't fair to you guys. I should have never been so cold and rude."

"I just thought you'd decided we were too nerdy to hang out with," Kevin said.

"Yeah, like you wanted to be part of the cool crowd and we weren't it," Matt said.

Marcie gave me a knowing look, then smirked. "I just thought the big gray bird freaked you out."

I laughed out loud, super hard. "Gayle is interesting," I said. "Anyway, I'm sorry, guys, and thank you for helping me find Spike. Want shortbreads?" I asked, pushing the plate closer to the trio.

Everyone dug in. Then I told Kevin and Matt something I'd wanted to for a long time. "By the way, Captain Janeway on *Star Trek: Voyager* is totally better than Captain Picard on *Star Trek: Next Gen*."

The room erupted in debate, but I held my own and defended Marcie completely.

Two apologies down, I thought. *One more to go. And it has to be perfect.*

37

A few weeks later, it was the middle of March—and time for the pet talent show. Well, almost. The day before the show, the weather in Frederick was particularly warm, teasing us of the spring to come. I had officially made Wilma my assistant for the show, and we'd been practicing with Spike every chance we got. Aunty Jacq had ordered us matching sweatshirts that read TEAM HEDGIE—in black and white, of course.

I still hadn't had a chance to formally apologize to Nick. I mean, I had told him I was sorry in Mr. Toliver's class the Tuesday after all the drama—and he'd said that we were good—but I hadn't had the chance to share anything with him. Now

I was going to school prepared, ready to do it right, though I wasn't sure the surprise I had planned would be enough.

After finding Spike, I'd decided not to care anymore about getting too close to my new friends. Some friends stayed in your life forever, and some came and went with a season. Just because the time you had with someone was short didn't make it any less important. It was important to be glad for the time we had together. Wilma had taught me that. Life was tricky.

It had also been time to change my hair. Too much had gone on over the past six months, and I needed a clean start, so I dyed it the deepest black I could find. I liked the purple and the red, but black . . . I think that suited me the best.

The decoration czar at school had also felt it was time for a change. There was no longer any pink and red to be found any-where—no #LOVEs, no valentines. In its place was pure luck. Green clover everywhere. Spring break was also coming up, and a new feeling of anticipation filled the hallways.

Wilma and I weren't immune to it as we walked into school together.

"TGIF," she said.

"Woot," I replied.

"See you after school." With a wave, she hustled off to her class. I didn't need to go to my locker just yet, so I went straight to Mr. Toliver's class. The door was unlocked, but there wasn't anyone inside. I walked to the back, hung my coat, and sat down. Then I pulled the book that Nick gave me out of my bag and waited.

Nick was the second person to arrive. He flashed his amazing smile my way. "Club Early Birds is in session," he said, dropping his bag by his seat and going to hang his coat.

"That's right," I said, giving him a real Rayna smile as he sat down. "So, Nick, I have something for you."

"You do?"

"Yep." I pulled the book out of my lap and placed it on my desk.

"Are you giving that back to me?"

"Not at all," I said. "Remember when we were at the gallery and I told you that in my family, when we apologize, we always share something? Tea or cocoa or whatever?"

"Right, like the jasmine in your aunt's painting."

"Exactly," I said. "You shared this book with me, and I wanted to tell you that I've read it from cover to cover. You were right. Totally depressing book. But not *just* depressing—it made me angry, too. No one ever teaches us any of this. I knew that we didn't have as many buffalo as we once did, but I didn't know it was because they were killed off to steal land and make Native people go hungry. And I had only ever heard of the Trail of Tears in school, but I didn't know that there were lots of trails by lots of people all over North America."

Nick listened quietly, watching me as I spoke.

"I know I'm not actually bringing you tea or anything, but I wanted you to know that I'm really sorry for pushing you away, especially after you shared so much with me and were so kind. And I don't just want to know about the history in this book. I want to know about Nick and his family."

Suddenly, Nick bolted up from his chair.

Oh no, did I offend him?

"Well, are you going to stand up so I can give you a big hug or what?" he asked, looking down on me with his warm turquoise eyes. "If you're cool with getting hugs."

"I'm cool," I said, grinning. I stood up and gave him a hug.

"You'll have to tell me all about being Italian, too, okay? It's not fair that Wilma is the one that gets fed all the time."

I chuckled. "Deal," I said.

Our conversation was interrupted by kids pouring into the classroom and hanging up their coats. It was loud and boisterous, like most Fridays. But there was a peaceful calm between me and Nick. And I was grateful.

38

Wilma and I had made lots of signs that read QUIET, PLEASE to go around the official Hedgie Gym we'd built for Spike for the talent show. But until it was time for us to go on, the hall was loud and full of barking, meowing, and chirping.

The fundraiser had originally been planned as an outdoor event in the little amphitheater at the park, but it was pouring rain outside, so the National Guard had generously offered their building to host.

A large rectangular room had been set up for the event. On one of the long sides, an area was designated as the "stage." Three sections of chairs faced it. If all the seats were filled, it would be quite an audience! To the right of the stage was a landing spot for all the talent and their props. Wilma and I hung around Spike's Hedgie Gym. Chairs squeaked on floors as onlookers found a place to watch the show.

"Too bad animals can't read," Wilma said. "Even if everyone in here gets as silent as the grave, their yippy mutts and yowling cats may still distract our little champion."

"It is what it is." I sighed, giving Spike a few pats through his new carrying pouch. It looked like the one he'd had when I'd lost him, but I'd deemed that one bad luck and refused to use it anymore. This one was fresh from the pet store, and I'd thoroughly checked the zippers over and over again to make sure that there would be no lost hedgehogs.

I spotted Kevin and Matt across the big room, carrying in Gayle's cage covered in a large sheet. They sported matching shirts with a screen-printed photo of Gayle on them looking pretty happy for a parrot.

"Is Gayle still saying 'To infinity and beyond' in your voice?" Wilma asked.

"Yep. I went over there yesterday to see how things were going. It's so creepy to have an animal sound just like you."

I felt a furry creature at my feet. Mr. Unega had come over to say hi! He was attached to a long leash that led to where Nick was, fifteen feet away. He flashed me his warm smile. I grinned back. A real one. Not a courteous half smile.

But someone was still missing. "Have you seen Marcie yet today?" I asked Wilma.

"No, but I'm sure she's here somewhere. I'll go have a look around."

"Cool," I said.

Nick slowly shortened Mr. Unega's leash and closed the distance between us. "How's Spike doing today? You feel ready?"

"I think so. Plus, it's for a good cause, right? Even if he just curls up in a ball and sits there, everyone still paid for a ticket."

"True that," Nick said. "How are things with your mom? Have you heard anything yet?"

"Nope. Just that we are supposed to have a family meeting when we get home today. That's usually when they give me a list of reasons why moving is a good thing."

"I remember those," Nick said. "Looks like they're passing out the lineup for the show. I'll go grab one for us."

As Nick and Mr. Unega went over to get the list from a

VFW volunteer, I looked around the room at the community that had gathered. On one side, very elderly veterans were given seats right at the front. Some were in wheelchairs. All had on baseball hats with the division they had served in printed across the front. I may have complained a lot about the army, but seeing everyone in the room, I also realized what an extended community my family had.

Where are they, anyway? I wondered, looking around for them but coming up empty.

Nick came back with the lineup. "Looks like Marcie and Daisy are up first, followed by Matt, Kevin, and Gayle, then me and Mr. Unega, and you and Spike. But there are a bunch more kids going before us, so I guess we can chill and watch for now?"

"Sounds good," I said. We made our way to some chairs near the props with a decent view of the "stage."

"Hey, Rayna, how is that new pouch working out for you?" a voice said from the chair behind me.

I turned around to see Justin sitting with a very tall, elderly woman who wore a beautiful blue scarf.

"Hey, Justin. I didn't know you were coming today. The

pouch is amazing. Spike really loves how soft—and secure—it is," I said.

"That's great. This is my grandma, Eleanor Charles," he said, gesturing to the woman in the scarf. "Grandma, this is Rayna. She has a hedgehog."

"Nice to meet you, Rayna. I do love those little hedgies. Can't wait to see yours perform!"

As I smiled at Justin's grandma, I finally spotted Mom and Aunty Jacq in the crowd. They were sitting in the aisle seats on the same side of the room as the elderly veterans. I watched Mom get up from her seat and help a nice-looking man in an old tan suit with his oxygen tank and then sit back down. Our eyes met and she gave me a thumbs-up. I smiled back. I was still a little angry at her. But I also knew she was trying, and she was still my mom.

Wilma plopped down in the seat next to me with Marcie and a very winded Daisy in tow. "I thought we'd get some extra practice in, but then Daisy took off running toward a squirrel she saw on the edge of the parking lot."

Nick and I chuckled. Marcie, on the other hand, did not find it funny. "I hope she doesn't get distracted!"

"I think we're all in the same boat," Wilma said, pointing to the chaos around us.

Marcie froze. I turned to see what or who she was looking at. Was it Justin? She slowly sat in the seat on the other side of Wilma and stared straight ahead. Wilma and I exchanged a look. She shrugged.

The crowd quickly quieted down as a young woman wearing fatigues led a German shepherd onto the stage. The German shepherd took a seat next to the woman's feet. "Thank you all for coming out this afternoon in support of our retired K9 warriors," she said into her microphone.

Everyone clapped, and I could swear the German shepherd was smiling.

The emcee continued. "These brave four-legged warriors have been serving our country since 1942. Back then, they were called 'Dogs of Defense' and their first assignment was serving in North Africa. Since then, K9 units have served selflessly and bravely for generations. This beautiful girl is one of our recent retirees, Ladybear. She served with the allied forces in Afghanistan and Iraq, detecting explosives. A dog's nose is fifty times more sensitive than ours, and with loyalty and talent, Ladybear has used her nose to save numerous lives."

Everyone clapped again.

"To ensure that dogs like Ladybear get the support and care they need in retirement, a few of our local kids have come together to entertain you all with their own special animal friends to raise money for their needs. Are you ready to see what they can do?"

Now the crowd was on its feet, clapping and whistling wildly.

"Okay, first up, we have Megan and her bullfrog, Rupert."

I watched a bullfrog leap, a dog sit up and beg, a cat chase a laser around the floor—which brought on tons of laughter from the crowd. Finally, it was time for my friends and me to take the stage.

Marcie led Daisy in front of the crowd, and asked for three volunteers to join them. Two teenage boys and an elderly woman volunteered. She placed them at intervals across the stage, holding Hula-Hoops in different directions and varied heights. Then she positioned Daisy on one end of the hoops while she sat on the other. When she held out a bouncy blue ball and said, "Daisy, get the ball!" Daisy immediately jumped into action, flying through the hoops one at a time, grabbing the ball in her mouth, and running back through the hoops to her starting place. She was probably the fastest dog in Frederick!

Next up, Kevin and Matt wheeled Gayle and her cage out into the middle of the stage, along with two stools. What transpired next was a comedy routine I wasn't expecting, with the twins asking Gayle questions, and Gayle quoting movie lines in response. The routine ended with her shouting, "TO INFINITY AND BEYOND!" in my voice.

I laughed so hard I started coughing. Gayle gave me the side-eye, and said, "It's okay," followed by "Want some water?"

Now it was Nick and Mr. Unega's turn. Nick took Mr. Unega through all kinds of tricks. He sat, rolled over, fetched, shook hands—all the regular stuff—then some music began. It had a modern sound, but I also heard drumming that reminded me of videos of powwows that Nick had shown me. Nick began bouncing on one foot and then the next—the standard dance of middle school boys everywhere. Mr. Unega followed suit, mirroring Nick. He turned when Nick turned, copying his every move. When the music stopped, both turned to the audience and took a bow. The crowd went wild.

Finally, it was Spike's turn. I looked over at Wilma and she nodded, signaling she was ready. We carried out Spike's Hedgie Gym with its quiet signs to the stage area. Everyone took the hint and stilled themselves.

Wilma opened up the can of worms we'd brought and grabbed the long tweezers while I pulled Spike out of his carrying pouch and sat him down on the table. He sniffed around a little bit and then put an ear in my direction.

"Hi, Spike, how are you doing, buddy?"

Spike's nose twitched and he turned toward me.

"Why don't you come over here, Spike? Come over here to me."

Spike paddled across the table to me. Wilma leaned in with the tweezers and a juicy worm that Spike devoured hungrily. The audience chuckled, but Wilma pointed at one of our signs and everyone quieted back down.

I moved to the other end of the gym. "Spike, why don't you come over here?"

Spike waddled back across the table to my voice. Wilma supplied him with another tasty worm.

I walked behind the table to its middle. "Spike, it's time for our big finale, you ready?"

Wilma put another worm on the end of the tweezers.

"Spike, let's show everyone how dogs aren't the only pets who can learn new tricks."

The room was silent with anticipation.

"Spike, roll over."

Spike rolled over.

Everyone gasped. Wilma provided a worm.

"Now, Spike, come back over here."

Spike began waddling toward me.

"Stop, Spike."

Spike stopped midway across the table.

"Spike, stay."

Spike stayed, right there in the middle. Even when Wilma held TWO juicy worms nearby, Spike stayed.

Wilma and I took a bow, and the crowd erupted in applause. I put Spike back in his carrying pouch, and checked the zipper three times to make sure it was closed before we headed back to our seats.

When the show was over, the crowd trickled into another part of the building for refreshments. Our gang of six huddled around my Hedgie Gym table and greeted audience members who came by to compliment us. Spike, in his trusty carrying pouch, soaked up the attention. There were tons of oohs and aahs over the little guy.

All of a sudden, Marcie leaned over to me and said in a loud whisper, "He's coming over here."

I looked up to see Justin and his grandma approaching us.

"Yeah . . . ?"

"He's like . . . he's like . . ."

"Tall?" I asked.

"Cute," Marcie said.

"He's sixteen and totally too old for you."

"Of course," she whispered.

"But he's also really nice and loves animals."

"Right," she said, gathering herself.

When Justin and his grandma reached our table, Marcie stood up a bit taller.

"Did you like the show?" I asked them.

"It was marvelous!" Ms. Charles exclaimed.

"I'm so glad you liked it. Justin, Ms. Charles, this is my friend Marcie. She's, like, the smartest person I know."

"Nice to meet you, Marcie," Justin said.

"Great show, dear," Ms. Charles said.

"Thanks!"

Someone stopped at the table to greet Justin and Ms. Charles.

Marcie leaned over and whispered in my ear, "He may be too old for me, but it doesn't hurt to dream."

I chuckled, giving Marcie a high five, then quickly turned my attention back to Ms. Charles.

We chatted for a bit longer, then I went to find my mom and Aunty Jacq. They were by the door of the building, both holding plates full of snacks and glasses of iced tea.

"There she is," Aunty Jacq said. "The rain has completely lifted. Want to sit outside with us at a picnic table while we eat?"

Oh no. Are they going to talk to me here? Now?

"Um, okay," I said.

The picnic table was still a little wet, but the sun was shining and the air smelled like fresh grass.

Here we go, I thought. *This is where they tell me we're moving to San Diego.*

I sat down, my hands going cold and clammy.

Aunty Jacq set the plates down in front of us. "I tried to get a little bit of everything. Oh, and Rayna, I brought you this from home." Aunty Jacq reached into her jacket pocket and pulled out a grape soda.

"Thanks, Aunty Jacq," I said, giving her a grateful grin.

I had to hand it to them. They were doing everything they could to ease the blow.

"Family meeting time," Mom said.

"Obviously," I smirked. I was trying to be lighthearted, but inside I was filled with absolute dread. Even though I knew what was coming and had accepted it, I was still scared. And there was still that anger stirring in my heart toward my mom. Would I be able to hold it in?

Aunty Jacq and Mom both looked pleasantly happy and not at all concerned. I was especially surprised that Aunty Jacq felt that way. How could she possibly be okay with moving?

Mom cleared her throat. "As you know, I've been weighing what the next step of my career should be. And after talking through my options with my superior officer and his superior officer, it looks like for the next few weeks, I'll be in San Diego," she said.

Here it came, the list of amazing things that awaited me in California—promises I'd rather she didn't make.

"For the first two weeks, I will be training a new sergeant."

"Okay," I said, wiping my hands on my jeans under the table.

"After that, it'll be my turn to train for a new job." *And there it is.* My heart was breaking. "A civilian job here at Fort Meade."

"Wait. What?" I asked, searching her face for more of an explanation.

"I have decided not to re-up. Your good ol' mom here is becoming a civilian—well, I'll be one in two months when all the bureaucracy is finally complete."

I couldn't believe what I was hearing.

"Angel," Aunty Jacq said, reaching her hand out to me across the table. "We're staying."

I felt like the wind had been knocked out of me. I was in shock—happy shock, but shock nonetheless. As Mom and Aunty Jacq came around to my side of the table, I stood up and hugged them both. Tears gathered in my eyes, but not the angry or sad kind. The kind full of amazement and relief and joy.

"We're staying," I repeated.

"That's right, Angel," Mom said. "Welcome home."

After our hug, I gave them a sheepish look and said, "I know this is a family moment and everything, but—"

"Go tell your friends, Angel," Mom said.

"Thank you! I'll be back later!" I yelled, already almost to the door of the building. I ran straight for my friends, who were still over by the pet prop table.

"Everybody," I said, taking a deep breath, "I'm staying! My mom's taking a job as a civilian at Fort Meade."

"Word," Kevin and Matt said in unison. They slapped each other a high five.

Marcie and Wilma jumped on me, hugging me tight. "That's great, girl with a hedgehog. That's really great," Wilma said.

When I looked up at Nick, I'd never seen him smiling so big. And it wasn't because Mr. Unega was nipping at my feet. That dog had a way of sneaking up on you. I bent down and let him slobber me with kisses.

And for once, I didn't feel like I didn't belong. I felt welcomed. Welcomed home.

39

Spring had definitely sprung. I'd swapped my heavy coat for my favorite denim jacket with its Day of the Dead skull on the back and a soft crimson-red hoodie. I was also sporting some new Converse, hand-painted with a new spiky design. There were still skulls, of course. But amid the skulls was a tiny, prickly hedgehog . . . and his worms.

Gross. Hysterical. Awesome.

Everyone at school seemed to have a little spring fever, and riding on the bus with the crew was loud, ridiculous, and full of jokes. Kevin and Matt argued. Marcie decided who was right, and Wilma and I scrolled through her smartphone in search of the very best skull earrings. When we found the perfect ones, Wilma got in the zone, hunting for a pair at a price that would fit her allowance.

While she shopped, I gazed out the window as the houses and buildings and trees of Frederick passed by. This was my town, my community. I had been here less than a year and already felt proud of it.

It was also the perfect place for Aunty Jacq. Now she could settle into the artist community around her and spread her wings. It would be a little while before Mom was home and commuting to Fort Meade, but when she was back for good, I had a feeling she was going to plant the best garden ever. She would truly be Sergeant First Class of Backyard Gardening.

When the bus pulled up along the side of FMS, we all began filing out.

"See you at lunch, Rayna?" Marcie asked.

"Yep. And I brought treats from Aunty Jacq," I said, patting my backpack.

"Nice," Kevin and Matt said in unison as they sprang from the bus.

Wilma had already disappeared. *How does she do that?* I knew I'd see her later anyway. Her dad was going to be home that night, and said she could ask me over for pizza. I knew things weren't the best over there, but it looked like they were beginning to spend a little more time together.

"Oh, Marcie, wait," I shouted to the gang up ahead. "Do you need help setting up your experiment for the science fair next week?"

"That would be amazing, Rayna! But it's top secret till then, okay?"

"Of course!" I said, then lowered my voice to a whisper. "How is your new robot, anyway? Have a name for it yet?"

"Not yet," she whispered back, "but Daisy hates it." Then she ran ahead to catch up with Kevin and Matt.

"There you are," a voice said. I turned around and was met with a set of familiar turquoise eyes and an amazing smile. "I'm really glad you get to stay."

"That's what you've been telling me," I said, teasing.

"What I mean is, I think gifts are in order. You know, to celebrate." He held up a large green bag that looked like it had seen better days. "I ordered them online, and they didn't come wrapped. But I found this to put them in—I think it might be from Christmas?"

I laughed and took the bag, looking down at my shoes for courage. Even after all this time, staring into Nick's eyes could make me feel like jelly, and I didn't want to fall over in the parking lot. I opened up the bag to see what it carried. Inside was a brand-new set of black Converse sneakers.

"Thought you'd like to commemorate the occasion by painting something . . . new? Some of your sneakers are downright terrifying. Maybe some flowers with your skulls or something?"

I beamed from ear to ear. Nick truly was a good human. A thoughtful human. A thoughtful, cute human.

"Thank you," I said, almost in a whisper.

He stepped forward and took both my hands, the bag dangling between our fingers. I looked up at him then; his eyes were warm and peaceful. Then, ever so gently, he leaned in and gave me a small, sweet kiss.

My face broke out into an uncontrollable smile.

"I have to make a quick run to the library to drop off a book. See you in Mr. Toliver's class?" Nick asked.

I nodded, still smiling, and watched him head off through the school doors, his long braid gently swaying behind him.

I looked around. There were very few people left outside. *I better get to class!*

And with that, I walked on air into the building.

Acknowledgments

I would like to thank my editor Jenne Abramowitz for seeing me write this book before I did. Her deft skills as an editor are truly magical. Pure sorcery. I hope to be more like her. I would also like to thank my agent, Linda Camacho, whose wisdom and support have meant the world to this type A Indigenous author.

Along the way this book has had many Sherpas, thank you to all the readers, experts, and guides who helped me bring this story to life.

Thank you to my nation, the Cherokee Nation, my elders, friends, and family. You all are the true inspiration for this book. To be friends with your family and to make families from friends, that is a true blessing and I am grateful.

And to Lenny Ciotti, my partner, my love, thank you.

Find more reads you will love . . .

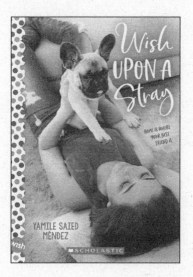

María Emilia's life turns upside down when she and her family immigrate from Argentina to the US. Luckily, she has the company of a dog in the neighborhood who loves to listen to her sing. It turns out the sweet pup belongs to María Emilia's new neighbor, Donovan, who invites her to join his band. But can Emilia find her new voice without losing herself?

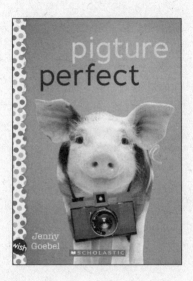

All Grace wants is a puppy—someone to love who'll make her new stepfather's house feel like home. But the surprise waiting for her Christmas morning isn't soft and furry—it's a pig! Will Grace figure out a way to make him part of the family? Or will this adorable troublemaker tear them apart?

Avery can sing, but hates singing *in front of people*. She likes to stay backstage at her new school, which is where, to her surprise, she finds a cat! As she sings to the stray one day, her crush, Nic, overhears her and ropes Avery into auditioning for the school's musical. When she lands the lead role, Avery knows she should be excited, but mostly she's terrified. Can Phantom the cat help her through her stage fright?

Have you read all the *wish* books?

☐ *Clementine for Christmas* by Daphne Benedis-Grab

☐ *Snow One Like You* by Natalie Blitt

☐ *Allie, First at Last* by Angela Cervantes

☐ *Gaby, Lost and Found* by Angela Cervantes

☐ *Lety Out Loud* by Angela Cervantes

☐ *Keep It Together, Keiko Carter* by Debbi Michiko Florence

☐ *Just Be Cool, Jenna Sakai* by Debbi Michiko Florence

☐ *Alpaca My Bags* by Jenny Goebel

☐ *Pigture Perfect* by Jenny Goebel

☐ *Sit, Stay, Love* by J. J. Howard

☐ *Pugs and Kisses* by J. J. Howard

☐ *Pugs in a Blanket* by J. J. Howard

☐ *The Love Pug* by J. J. Howard

☐ *Girls Just Wanna Have Pugs* by J. J. Howard

☐ *Best Friend Next Door* by Carolyn Mackler

☐ *11 Birthdays* by Wendy Mass

☐ *Finally* by Wendy Mass

☐ *13 Gifts* by Wendy Mass

☐ *The Last Present* by Wendy Mass

☐ *Graceful* by Wendy Mass

☐ *Twice Upon a Time: Beauty and the Beast, the Only One Who Didn't Run Away* by Wendy Mass

☐ *Twice Upon a Time: Rapunzel, the One with All the Hair* by Wendy Mass

- [ ] *Twice Upon a Time: Robin Hood, the One Who Looked Good in Green* by Wendy Mass
- [ ] *Twice Upon a Time: Sleeping Beauty, the One Who Took the Really Long Nap* by Wendy Mass
- [ ] *True to Your Selfie* by Megan McCafferty
- [ ] *Blizzard Besties* by Yamile Saied Méndez
- [ ] *Random Acts of Kittens* by Yamile Saied Méndez
- [ ] *Wish Upon a Stray* by Yamile Saied Méndez
- [ ] *Playing Cupid* by Jenny Meyerhoff
- [ ] *Hedge over Heels* by Elise McMullen-Ciotti
- [ ] *Cake Pop Crush* by Suzanne Nelson
- [ ] *Macarons at Midnight* by Suzanne Nelson
- [ ] *Hot Cocoa Hearts* by Suzanne Nelson
- [ ] *You're Bacon Me Crazy* by Suzanne Nelson
- [ ] *Donut Go Breaking My Heart* by Suzanne Nelson
- [ ] *I Only Have Pies for You* by Suzanne Nelson
- [ ] *Shake It Off* by Suzanne Nelson
- [ ] *Pumpkin Spice Up Your Life* by Suzanne Nelson
- [ ] *A Batch Made in Heaven* by Suzanne Nelson
- [ ] *Confectionately Yours: Save the Cupcake!* by Lisa Papademetriou
- [ ] *Pizza My Heart* by Rhiannon Richardson
- [ ] *My Secret Guide to Paris* by Lisa Schroeder
- [ ] *Switched at Birthday* by Natalie Standiford
- [ ] *Clique Here* by Anna Staniszewski
- [ ] *Double Clique* by Anna Staniszewski
- [ ] *Meow or Never* by Jazz Taylor
- [ ] *Revenge of the Angels* by Jennifer Ziegler

Read the latest *wish* books!